I0673308

High Noon Justice

~ *A Christian Fiction Novel*

Shakira R. Thompson

BELIEVER'S CHOICE
MEDIA

Advanced Praise for *High Noon Justice*

"Shakira has captured the essence of what so many of us have faced in the vicissitudes of living a happy, normal life. Reading this book has taken me through a myriad of emotions. I was able to reflect and laugh, get angry and cry, remember, smile, and praise. Sometimes people lose sight of the true identity and original concept of Christ and the Christ life in exchange for their own desires. When we encounter the people who have altered the original plan, the outcomes can make us feel weak and defeated. But thanks be to God, who has given us the victory and hope, revealed truth wins over deception every time."

DR. DIANE CLARK, *Kingdom Life Ministries International, Inc.* www.kingdomlifejax.org

"When I think of *High Noon Justice*, I think mesmerizing. Once I started reading, I was immediately drawn in to the stories of each character. I couldn't wait to find out what would happen next. Shakira is a master storyteller. Once you pick up this book, you won't be able to put it down."

DR. NADIA BROWN, *Doyenne Leadership Institute* www.doyenneleadership.com

as

"Transparent! More than just a novel, I felt every word unfold a scene in a movie. *High Noon Justice* opened a can many want to avoid. From the beginning scene, it is Christian Reality!"

DEE LEE, Christian Comedian, *Host of the Dee Lee Show,* www.thedeeleeshow.com

"In *High Noon Justice*, Fernandina Beach native, Shakira R. Thompson has written a fast-paced and inspirational novel filled with rich characters and a powerful message that while we may not always understand God's plan, we must always trust in it."

SIAN PERRY, *Fernandina Beach   News-Leader,* www.fbnewsleader.com

"This book hit so close to home in more ways than one! Riveting and unpredictable, yet realistic and brilliantly written. Shakira Thompson taps into the heartbeat of a "secret society," offering a peak into the inner happenings of a world most will never see or experience. You will read on the edge of your seat! Fantastic read!"

SHAUNA HARRISON, Co-Pastor *of New Beginnings Church - Orlando*
www.nborlando.com

"I realized in reading *High Noon Justice* that this is the first fiction book I've ever read. I'm not saying this because she's my daughter but this book pulled me in and captivated me from the start. Now, because she is my daughter, I will say that I'm extremely proud!"

LAVERNE F. MITCHEL, CEO of *Women of Power,*
www.womenofpowerinc.org

High Noon Justice

Printed in the United States of America

Titles are available at special discounts for bulk purchases by corporations, institutions, and other organizations.

Believer's Choice Media
P.O. Box 2131
Yulee, FL 32041
www.shakirabelieves.com

High Noon Justice
Edited by: Natoya Walker Alee
Designed by: Ivey Media Group, LLC / www.iveymediagroup.com

Library of Congress Congress Control Number: 2014913934
ISBN: 978-0-9906725-0-0 (p); 978-0-9906725-1-7 (digital)

Scripture quotations are taken from the *Holy Bible*, King James and Common English Bible Versions.

High Noon Justice is a work of fiction. All characters and places appearing in this work are fictitious. Any resemblance to real persons, living or dead, places, establishments, events, organizations, and/or locations is purely coincidental and a product of the author's mind.

First Printing, 2014

*To my ignition starter,
my guiding star,
and my little fire cracker.*

_____

ACKNOWLEDGEMENTS

I'm sure you will agree with me that at some point in time or another, trusting God can seem like a daunting task but little bit by little bit I'm learning to trust Him day by day and if I can do it, so can you.

Everything that I've ever experienced in my life has led me to this point. While most of it I didn't understand at the time, it's now beginning to make sense.

I have to first thank God, my Savior, who showed me the real meaning of Hebrews 12:6-8 (**AMP**):

"6 For the Lord corrects and disciplines everyone whom He loves, and He punishes, even scourges, every son whom He accepts and welcomes to His heart and cherishes.

7 You must submit to and endure [correction] for discipline; God is dealing with you as with sons. For what son is there whom his father does not [thus] train and correct and discipline?

8 Now if you are exempt from correction and left without discipline in which all [of God's children] share, then you are illegitimate offspring and not true sons [at all]."

If I don't know anything else, I know right now that the Lord loves me, He's proved it many times over and I'm eternally grateful.

Words cannot express how grateful I am to my husband, Keith M. Thompson and our beautiful little girls, my pride and joy. I appreciate you all for allowing me to fulfill destiny in the earth. Each of you are a tremendous blessing to me and I couldn't have done any of this without your support.

To Eric Ivey of the Ivey Media Group, thank you for designing an amazing book cover, I appreciate your patience and professionalism in dealing with me to take this project to another level. Every joint does supply and you demonstrated that with your design.

Thanks to Natoya Walker Alee, your editorial touch added some of the missing elements needed to bring this project more alive. Thank you for not holding back.

To the "Shakira's Sweethearts," my number one supporters. You've done it all, from being beta readers taking time out of your busy schedules to read the initial manuscript and provide me with invaluable feedback, to spreading the word about *High Noon Justice,* but most importantly, keeping me lifted up in prayer. I have nothing but love for each and everyone one of you and I speak God's choice blessings over you.

To ever reader, reviewer, bookstore, book club, friend or foe, thank you for all of your ongoing support. People do not have to do anything for you and I don't take what you do and have done for granted. I am truly grateful.

If I've forgotten anyone, charge it to my head and not my heart.

Thank you and May God Bless!

PROLOGUE

"**Y**ou were supposed to love me. Cherish me. Protect me. You promised...."

"I do...I did, or at least, I thought I did."

"What on earth does that mean – at least, you thought you did."

"If you didn't, you never should have married me!"

The shouts, the slams, the crashing from treasured ornaments against the walls filled the Montgomery home for hours.

Carson Montgomery was finding his stride in ducking from trying to miss the projectile objects being thrown at him by his wife, Scarlett.

Unable to understand what was happening to her in that moment, the internal sensations she felt, the mental responses she thought of, a wide range of emotions engulfed her, "How dare you? How could you do this to me, you selfish, ungrateful, son of a -?"

Putting up one hand and interrupting his wife, "Now you hold on a minute Scarlett..."

"Hold on? Hold on, you want me to hold on when you just informed me you're filing for a divorce? If I didn't know it before, I certainly know it now, you are one self-centered individual. Everything I've done for you and this family, and you're telling me, it's over? Oh, and let's not forget, you're supposed to be a man of God, right?" The sneering from Scarlett cut deep, "What part of Ephesians 5:25 do you not understand? Somehow, this doesn't feel very Godly, Pastor Mont-gom-ery?[1]"

Scarlett looked at Carson through eyes that seemed to be glowing, the tears and the snot flowed from her face onto the floor. This was the first time in hours, Scarlett was showing signs of slowing down and the appearance of a small break gave way for Carson to take control of the situation.

Carson folded back his starched long sleeves as he paced the floor, searching for the right way to deliver such wrong news.

"You see Scarlett, I did love you, or so I thought. At the time I met you, I was getting pressure from my parents and other mentors that it was time to find a wife. The thing is, I wasn't really ready. But you know my story, my legacy, and family history; if I was to begin taking over the leadership at the church, I needed to have a wife and start a family. Either I had to choose a wife or they were going to do it for me. So I chose you. I was hoping to get all of my needs met by you - sexually, emotionally, physically, I was looking for you to make me be ready for marriage. I needed you to fix me, make me a better man and you didn't."

Scarlett's heart seemed to freeze, then pound as she sat and listened to the disgraceful display of her husband's revelations. A slow, disbelieving shake of the head was the only thing moving on her stiffened petite frame.

---

[1] **Ephesians 5:25**: *"Husbands, love your wives, even as Christ also loved the church, and gave himself for it."*

Carson E. Montgomery IV, the epitome of a child born to that of a preacher man, walked both sides of the fence in life. From the moment of his birth he was groomed for ministry and leadership, he would represent the fourth generation of Montgomery men to lead Wondrous Works Tabernacle Fellowship, a 25,000 member multi-cultural church. Extremely charming, yet conniving, he was known to have a reputation with the female congregants.

His religious heritage subconsciously granted him levels of superiority.

There were reports and sightings of him in VIP areas of places like cigar lounges, sex shows, and strip clubs. Whenever these reports would surface the ministry would reduce them to mere rumors, attacks from people wanting to harm the good name of the family and the ministry. With long-standing traditions, influence as well as affluence within the community, people tended to believe whatever the church said. His pedigree also seemed to protect him.

Carson's dramatic monologue continued, "It's been five years and you still haven't produced me a baby to present to my family and the congregation. If you were unable to help me be better and then also not give me children, then what good are you to me?"

The room began to spin and close in on Scarlett, adrenaline spiking through her body caused her skin to tingle and her breath to be short. Not before letting out, "Did it ever occur to you that because you've sucked out all of the life from me, I didn't have any left to bring forth a life?"

Carson flapped his hand in dismissal towards Scarlett. "I knew it had to be you because we both know I put it down, you just haven't been picking up what I've been putting down."

"I'm your wife and I'm not going anywhere, we are going to work this out. Oh and don't get it twisted, all you've been putting down ain't all that great. So you might want to check yourself."

Carson's deliberate eyebrow raise and tilt of the head, signaled to Scarlett more was coming. Pulling down his glasses on his sharp nose and looking over the rims with a harrowing gaze, Scarlett definitely knew he had more up his sleeve.

"Uh Scarlett, I think others would tend to disagree with you on that and just so you know, we will not be working anything out. Listen to me, I'm going to lead this church and I need someone other than you to help me lead it. Hey, it's real simple, you and I just didn't work out."

"Carson, the man you presented yourself to be when we were dating is much different than who you turned out to be after we were married. Yet, I stayed with you. I've loved you in spite of your misgivings. For you to say what good am I to you; I've been everything to you. I'm a good wife and you know it. You know how I gave up everything to become your wife."

Scarlett's pleading was going in one of Carson's ears and coming out of the other, Scarlett's voice sounded like white noise to him until he heard, "Plus, please tell me this; if you married me for the church, how is now divorcing me going to help you in your pastoral pursuits?"

An expanded feeling filled his chest, enthused for what was about to come, "I'm glad you asked my dear. I've already spoken with our attorneys, Bishop, and the board of trustees and this is what's going to happen. Even though I'm the one wanting the divorce, you are going to be the one filing. I've already found another woman to marry and she and I will be getting married in about six months, time to allow me to heal from you leaving me. You are going to leave here and fade off into the sunset to never look back here ever again. You will change your last name and you will remove any ties from me, my family, and this ministry."

"Over my dead body Carson."

"We can have that arranged Scarlett, we just thought it would look better that you left me because you were unable to handle the pressures related to being in ministry rather than me becoming a widower. When you're in ministry at this level, it can take a toll on you and unfortunately, you never adjusted. The publicist for the church has already drafted the narrative to be released as soon as the divorce is final. She also wrote the letter you are going to leave me. Just so you know, we are on the fast track docket to have it finalized within a few days since one of our Trustees is a judge."

"I'll never agree to this Carson...wait a minute, let me get this straight, are you telling me that both Mama and Daddy Montgomery are going along with you on this? They are going to just let you do this to me?"

Seeing Carson pulling out the brown leather portfolio caused Scarlett to flashback to the days before her wedding where she signed the prenuptial agreement in the offices at the church. The only reason she signed was because she believed in the forever he promised. Based on the lavish wedding they were planning, she never thought in a million years anything written in those documents would come to pass, especially not within five years. He sold her a dream, a ticket he couldn't cash. To the core of who he was, he was emotionally bankrupt.

The rustling of the turning pages sickened Scarlett to her core, little did she know signing those documents she was signing over her life to this machine of a ministry.

"First of all, Bishop knows only a little bit but mother doesn't know anything, she'd never forgive me for this. I have to spin this in a way that works in my favor so that everyone believes me. Again, it's going to be better for her to believe my story that you left me and have her hate you instead of me...this plan is brilliant, right?

Scarlett was beside herself, unable to really absorb what was happening. She felt like she was watching a movie and she had the starring role.

"You know, the first thought I had was to go and do like the guys in the bible did back in the day and go and get me a couple of wives and a few concubines but since we don't live in Utah and I do have a heart, this plan seemed better."

"What has happened to you Carson...the stuff you are saying sounds crazy, even for you. What is going on? Who made you like this?"

Everything in Scarlett's view began to grow depressingly dark.

"Now, based on the prenuptial agreement you signed, there is a tiny little clause that states, if for whatever reason I deemed necessary to divorce you, I could, but we had to be married for at least five years and it's been five and a half. Should you accept the terms of the agreement, we will provide you with generous transitional support for a period of five years, the length of our marriage. After that, you're on your own, but you have to essentially forget everything about Wondrous Works and move on somewhere else."

Carson was consumed, he illustrated there was a method to his madness as he meticulously went over the details of Scarlett's departure.

"You will be removed from all ministry materials and we will shut off your cell phone service. All of your credit accounts will be canceled and I'll get all new bank cards and claim yours as lost. You will need to change your email accounts and come off of social media. You know what, just take this."

Carson slid a book over to Scarlett, "*How to Disappear and Start a New Life.*" "You are a smart girl, I'm sure you'll figure it out."

According to the document, there is also another clause that prohibits you from speaking about this, making any allegations, or bringing any lawsuits against us. We can't have you bringing any reproach upon the ministry now can we?"

The portfolio slammed shut, he pushed back from the table and walked over to his soon to be ex-wife.

Scarlett sat with her hands on her shaking head, repeating the word, "No." The questions swirled around in her head, "*What next? What now? Where do I go?*"

Carson loomed over her in an act of intimidation as she sobbed with her head on their table, "Scarlett, it's been nice but your reign as 'Mrs. Carson Montgomery' is up. Trust me on this Scarlett, God is in control, I've prayed and this is the will of God concerning you."

Doing a double take at Carson, feeling the need to verbalize her disbelief in what she was hearing, "Are you serious, are you even listening to the words coming out of your mouth? You are seriously trying to tell me this is the will of God concerning my life...incredible!"

"Yes Scarlett, I'm telling you, He's in control. In fact, He told me to give you the weekend to get your things together and remove yourself from the premises. So, when I come here on Sunday morning to get ready for church, I will expect you to be gone. You will leave quietly too and don't even think about going to see my parents. The Gulfstream private jet will take you wherever you want to go. You don't have to let me know where you end up, just leave your bank account information with my assistant and we'll take care of things on our end...good-bye."

The clock had struck midnight but this was no fairy tale. Life as she knew it was over, his arrogance had finally won, she chose to not let it bother her during the marriage but tonight, she felt mastered, conquered, defeated.

CHAPTER 1

"**S**o, today's the big day huh?"
The dent in the bed caused the covers to fly up over Scarlett's head as she rolled over herself to answer her father, "Good morning daddy. I guess it all depends on who you ask."

"Your mother is cooking up a storm in that kitchen this morning, she ran to the store for a quick second so I thought I'd come in and check on y'all. It's pouring down outside, I should have gone but you know your mother. She thinks I would have gotten the wrong thing. How are you holding up baby girl?"

Sitting up in the bed and rubbing her five-and-a-half-month belly, Scarlett let out a deep sigh, "We are doing fine...you know what daddy, it is what it is and you probably would have gotten the wrong thing."

The two shared a brief laugh.

"I appreciate what y'all are trying to do and I truly, truly love you for it but I'd actually rather not dwell on what this day is supposed to represent. Is it possible for us to treat it like any other day rather than my trifling behind ex-husband's wedding day?"

Placing a loving hand on Scarlett's shoulder, her father, George Watson, Sr. began to speak, "I -."

"Don't interrupt me daddy."

Scarlett pounded the floral colored queen-sized comforter, "I don't want to have to be reminded about how everyone thinks I abandoned my husband and filed for divorce. I would have thought someone there who knew me would question that but nothing. Hook, line, and sinker, everybody believed that cockamamie story. He got away with it, he won. Daddy, I don't want to think about how he is going to stand before God and man and profess his undying love and devotion to that woman. She's taking over my life. It just doesn't seem fair, what did I ever do to deserve this? They're over there prospering and I'm here suffering. I'm a good person, right daddy? My whole world has been turned upside down and it's so hard to see my way through any of this. He doesn't even know where I am or that I'm pregnant. If he'd only waited a few weeks before kicking me out, he would've known we are expecting our first child."

Scarlett inquired of these injustices to her father, however, internally she was also questioning God.

Each rant contained a heightened movement and octave in her voice, Scarlett spoke through her teeth with seemingly forced restraint as she continued on with her father. "This day would be a whole lot better if the thoughts of that woman taking my place under false pretenses didn't consume me. He used me and then abused me, how could he be so cruel? I was his wife...his wife and he did this to me. I feel like he's shattered my life into a million pieces like a broken mirror. You know what, I simply don't want to think about any of this daddy...it hurts too badly."

George pulled Scarlett close against his shoulder. Burying her face into his supportive and compassionate embrace, she allowed herself to mourn the loss of her former life. When she left the Montgomery compound, she ordered the pilot to take her to the only place she knew she needed to be...with her parents.

George and his wife, Minta were not very fond of Carson. In every encounter with him they sensed he wore a badge of entitlement and they felt Scarlett was too young. Nevertheless, they supported their daughter's decision to marry him. Scarlett assured her parents she was marrying the man of her dreams, to her, Carson was her knight in shining armor. Only he turned out to be more of a nightmare that never stopped shining.

After the wedding, the once strong relationship Scarlett shared with her parents became weakened due to the infrequent times of communication. Living the lifestyle, ministry demands, and making appearances seemed to put a wedge between Scarlett and her parents.

Nevertheless, in her time of need, when she called, they answered. They had been there to help her through one of the darkest yet brightest times in her life.

Despite trying to start over in a new life and essentially a new identity, shortly after arriving in Jordan, Mississippi, Scarlett learned of the impending arrival of the continuation of the Montgomery lineage, a constant reminder of her past, she was pregnant with Carson Montgomery's baby.

The gravity of the entire situation bubbled out of her onto her father's ample shoulders, he held her closely and rocked her gently without judgment as she gave herself over to the range of emotional energy raging through her expanding body.

The familiar aroma of Minta's infamous breakfasts traveled into Scarlett's room signaling to them she'd arrived back from the store. When the two didn't emerge as they would normally, Minta entered the room.

Tears filled her eyes as she stood in the door frame watching a heart-wrenching, yet heart-warming scene. One hand found its way to cover her mouth as the other clutched her chest. The administration of love from an earthly father offered a glimpse of the amazing love our Heavenly Father has for His children[2]. However, seeing the pain and struggle from her only daughter overshadowed the precious moment between a father and daughter.

Minta grew up without a father so learning to identify and receive God as "Father" was hard for her but once she felt His amazing love for her, it was an undeniable love. Minta loved her children had an excellent father in George, she wanted that for them considering her own childhood.

Minta knew deep within her daughter's situation was a difficult one but not one she couldn't overcome and that no matter what, they would be there to support her through it all. Despite the uniqueness of the circumstances, George and Minta were beyond thrilled to be welcoming their first grandchild.

Settling alongside the bed, Minta's arms reached around her husband and her daughter, finding a spot on

----

[2] **1 John 3:1:** *"See what great love the Father has lavished on us, that we should be called children of God! And that is what we are! The reason the world does not know us is that it did not know him."*

Scarlett's head, Minta rested hers, "Get it out baby, that's right...you let it all out. Your daddy and I got you, we got your back baby, we're going to be here to hold you up and help you through this."

"Good morning mama."

"Morning sweetheart, alright now you get up and get yourself together, I'm sure by now my grandbaby is ready to eat. It has already stopped raining and it's turning out to be a beautiful day. What we aren't going to do is spend it pining away over someone who doesn't deserve it, what we will do is thank the Lord for all that He's doing in your life and in this situation and watch Him move the way He wants to."

Minta was known to not mince words, her no nonsense approach to life was appreciated by all she came in contact with and it definitely helped whip Scarlett into shape. Minta had a knack for getting you right together but she always did it with the word and in love and that's what made the difference. Prior to moving to Mississippi, she was a highly respectable woman in her home, church, and community. Nevertheless, as new transplants to the area, her direct personality was winning over the city of Jordan."

When deciding upon a location to relocate after George's early retirement, he expressed to Minta he wanted to return to his old stomping grounds and return to Jordan, where he'd gone to college.

Two weeks after he stopped working they packed up their belongings and traveled across the beltway to the "Soulful City."

The following week, Scarlett called.

CHAPTER 2

"**P**eople are starting to arrive son, are you getting nervous?"

Carson's pasted on smile indicated he wasn't fully present in the moment. Regina Montgomery took her son's hand, "It's okay to be happy son. I don't mean to bring it up but I know you're still hurting. Only the Lord knows why Scarlett did what she did by upping and leaving you and disconnecting from all of us. I was so hurt by what she did to not only you but to all of us...honestly, I'm still hurting. I still pray for her daily, I loved her like she was my own daughter."

Dapping her eyes with a delicate eyelet lace handkerchief, Regina tried to be an encourager to her son, despite her feelings. You say you've found someone, someone that'll love you, stand by, and support you in this ministry and I hope you're right about that."

By repositioning Carson's boutonniere, Regina hugged her son, he wore an unnatural stillness that was unfamiliar to her, "Son, you seem so nervous, are you alright? Listen, there's a lady waiting to become Mrs. Carson Montgomery, you better get yourself together. Now remember, I love you."

Closing his eyes and taking in a calming breath, his mother's scent calmed him, he simply replied, "I love you too; I'll see you out there."

Unbeknownst to First Lady Montgomery, Carson wasn't feeling nervous, the empty feeling in the pit of his stomach had been lingering and it wasn't caused by feelings of anxiety but guilt. Although, he could never let on to his mother the true source of his discontentment.

A knock at the door broke the trance Carson found himself in, "uh, yeah, come on in."

The groomsmen all entered acting hyper, telling jokes, and chest bumping with each other. They babbled and talked over the other as the group settled in together before leaving to take their positions in the church.

"You ready man, it's 'bout to go down in here today...again!" Christian, the middle son joked around slapping Carson on his back.

Carson did not seem amused; he was not enjoying the communal energy in the room. "I see you got jokes today, huh?"

"Dang, big bro...how 'bout you try and loosen up a bit, will you? So yeah, before I forget, I spoke briefly with Cayden-James today, he sends his love. He wishes he could be here."

The wedding planner beckoned for the tuxedoed quartet to follow her. They followed her to Bishop Montgomery's office to get him before going into the sanctuary. Bishop Montgomery was set to officiate and he was adorned in his ceremonial robe for the occasion. Not a word was spoken among the men, only a reverential nod to the Bishop.

The main auditorium was filled with over five hundred guests, family and friends of the couple to celebrate their new nuptials. Some were well-wishers, some were not, others were just plain nosey.

As the processional began, Carson found it hard to concentrate on his wedding. His mind began to wander back on the day six months prior from when he essentially destroyed Scarlett.

He never once took in the sights and smell of the thousands upon thousands of flowers draping the pews and columns. He overlooked the regal nature of the high-priced décor featuring all of the symbolisms associated with a wedding.

He did however, replay the scenario, his last night with Scarlett over and over in his mind until he heard the short blasts of the customary chords of Mendelssohn's most notorious, "Wedding March" and saw everyone stand to welcome the bride, Rebekkah Marie Hudson and her father, Daniel Hudson.

The doors flung opened to a revelation of glamour in a luxurious ruffled organza ball gown in brilliant white. Rebekkah's cinched waistband was heavily embellished and sparkled in the candlelight adorning each aisle. The sweetheart neckline of the dress flattered her body to the fullest, she could have easily graced the cover of a featured bridal magazine. The glorious image of Rebekkah snapped Carson back into reality and he began to tear up. Question is, what did the tears represent? Nevertheless, Rebekkah and her father eventually made their way to the altar where she joined hands with her future husband, Carson Eugene Montgomery, IV.

Whispering in her ear, "You look stunning."

Bishop Montgomery served in his official capacity and performed a beautiful ceremony of holy matrimony whereby he pronounced them, "Husband and Wife."

Giving the blessed proclamation, "Carson, you may now salute your bride."

The audience clapped and cheered as the couple took their first kiss as newlyweds. Triumphant, high-spirited praise music rung out through the building as the recessional was underway.

An extravagant, over-the-top reception immediately followed the ceremony beginning with a cocktail hour while the bridal party fulfilled their photographic obligations.

While some time had passed since Scarlett's departure, she and Carson were still a topic of conversation at the wedding. At different tables, one could overhear things such as –

"It's a darn shame how that girl just up and left him like that."

"I wonder whatever happened to First Lady Scarlett, does anyone ever hear from her?"

"I was at his first wedding, while this was a beautiful one, I think his first one was better."

"I think Carson is something else to deal with, I probably would have left his behind too."

"Let's see how long this one lasts."

"First Lady Scarlett had it all, she had everything and she walked off and left it all and Pastor C."

All of the conversations were quite colorful and varied depending upon the people seated at the table.

The conversations all turned towards the couple once the bridal party was introduced and the new Mr. and Mrs. Carson Montgomery was presented.

Carson escorted his lovely bride onto the dance floor where they enjoyed their first dance. Once the song was over, he grabbed the microphone, "I read a quote once that said; life is not measured by the amount of breaths you take but by the amount of times your breath has been taken away. I stand before you all and declare that today was one of those moments, my wife....my bride took my breath away. She has made me a happy man. I love her so much and I'm looking forward to spending the rest of my life with her. I love you Rebekkah Montgomery."

Carson pulled Rebekkah into him closer and kissed her deeply. The guests cheered them on.

"Now, with that being said, this is all well and good and fun and you all can continue to enjoy your time here at our reception but uh, me and my wife will be heading on out, we have some important matters to attend to...if you know what I mean." With a wink and smile he gathered up his new bride.

Bishop stood up quickly and grabbed the microphone from his son, "Well this isn't how I thought the night would go but hey, let's roll with it. Before you two lovebirds get out of here, your mother and I have an announcement. Honey, will you come?"

Bishop and First Lady Regina stood with locked arms together, "I'd like to announce that I've set a retirement date and I will be officially passing the mantle over to my eldest son, Carson. In six months, Pastor

Carson will formerly take over the leadership at Wondrous Works Tabernacle Fellowship."

Both couples hugged and turned to see a standing ovation.

Carson's announcement clearly caught Rebekkah by surprise but she gracefully said her goodbyes and followed her husband, hand-in-hand through the doors to the Artic White Rolls-Royce that awaited them outside.

Looking back one last time at her reception, the one she'd be missing out on, the first doubt filled her head, "*Oh my God, what have I gotten myself into?*"

CHAPTER 3

"**W**ell thank the Lord, we made it through to another weekend. See honey, no need to get stuck because every day you wake up, things are going to continue to get better. Have you gone on your walk yet?"

"Not yet mama, I just felt like lounging around for a bit this morning." Scarlett sipped on her herbal tea, blowing away the moist steam while reading the morning paper."

Minta continued talking with Scarlett overlooking the fact she was reading. "I love what you've been able to do with your blog in such a short period of time dear. More and more people are starting to join the program and I think it's been quite therapeutic for you."

With a slow and steady nod, Scarlett didn't skip a beat with her tea or reading.

"Mama, can you believe this, according to this article in the *Jordan Journal*, Jordan is one of the top ten most obese cities in the country."

Minta lifted her perfectly arched eyebrow, "Maybe that explains why more and more people are finding your site."

Scarlett moved to get more tea.

"You stay seated; I'll get that for you. Honey, I hope you're beginning to see some purpose in all that is happening."

Nestling herself back into the breakfast nook chair, Scarlett cocked her head to the side. "I don't get what you mean, as of yet, I don't see the purpose of any of this."

Minta placed the mug in front of Scarlett along with a bite for her to eat.

"Look at it Scarlett, your father and I relocate to this area looking for a new start into our retirement years where we know no one and then shortly thereafter you come here to us with your situation. You start walking every day, just you and God, walking and talking and it sparks an idea for you to create this site of yours. Now, you see that you are in a city where people need what you have to offer. Oh, and let's not forget this precious miracle you're carrying. Even though you still don't even look like you are expecting, with your tiny, little self. I'm ready to see your big 'ole baby bump."

Scarlett pondered on the words of her mother.

"Honey, what you are going through was never meant to destroy you. Yes, you got knocked down but you didn't get knocked out, you got up. Romans 8:28, is not just a cliché we quote in times of trouble, but it's a promise from God and girl, let me tell you something...all things are working together for you. This should be a lifestyle motto for the believer. No, we may not understand all of what He's doing. I believe God has a script written for us that only He knows about. It's not for us to know all of the particulars of the script, it is up to us however, to be flexible to the details though."

Minta's encouraging words changed Scarlett's posture she leaned in forward, sliding her chair in closer to her mother. "One thing I know mama, this baby saved my life. I've been angry and I've been sad. I've been frustrated and honestly, I've also been jealous of them at times. When I thought about losing my mind, I couldn't because I had to make sure and take care of myself for the sake of the baby."

"God knows all things honey. None of this is a surprise to Him. What you need to do is just chill out and wait for Him to act on your behalf."

"So mama, you really think God is up to something in this situation?"

"Of course I do and so do you, I hope when you're going on these walks with Him, you aren't doing all of the talking. I hope you're listening as well."

Scarlett wiped the corners of her mouth as she almost spit out the tea laughing at her mother's comment.

"I'm sure it's probably been a little difficult for you to walk and talk with Him since I've started going with you though."

"Well, it's been nice having you come along. I also have been enjoying my walking and talking with daddy too. You know what, now that you mention it, I believe the Lord has been talking to me. For the last several weeks I've been hearing in a very faint voice, I'm preparing you...I'm preparing you. I think that in my own despair, I hadn't been able to fully receive it or better yet, believe it."

Minta clapped her hands together, "Now see, that's what I'm talking about. Scarlett, you may not see it now but there is purpose in this trial you're going through. I believe God is going to use you in a mighty way. You have purpose and so does my grandbaby, we all do. You just wait and see."

George walked into the breakfast area where the ladies were talking and plopped a stack of mail in the center of the table.

"Hello there my lovely ladies. What are you two yapping about in here? Oh Scarlett, there is some mail in there for you sweetheart."

George was known to be somewhat of a jokester, he always kept the family laughing. Growing up, Scarlett and her younger brother, George, Jr. knew they had the funniest dad of all their friends.

As a newly retired, former bank president, trying to find the balance between once holding a prestigious and powerful position to getting acclimated to not working was not as easy as he thought it would be.

One of the ways he was spending his free time was on the golf course as one of the newest members of the country club in their community. Other times he'd leave the home without anyone knowing where he went.

"I'm going to go for a round of golf later today Scarlett, you want to come along with your dear old dad?"

"This is unbelievable."

George's head flinched backwards, "What is so unbelievable about you riding in a cart with me at the golf course?"

Scarlett dropped the letter she'd found in the stack of mail on the table, just as her mouth dropped open. It was her monthly statement for her transitional support.

Normally it's the same amount each month, sometimes she wouldn't even open the envelope. However, this time when she did, there was an increase of five thousand additional dollars to the already generous amount she received.

George picked up the letter and looked it over, "I see no issues here, how about you Minta?"

Crossing her hands over her chest, Scarlett questioned the motives, "*I wonder what this is all about? Why is he now sending me extra money?*"

Minta leaned over towards George to take a peek, "I'm with your daddy on this one; I see no issues here either. This is why I told you early on not to let what Carson did to you, make you sin and get on the wrong side of this. See because, guess what, the good guys do always win."

Trying not to allow her mind to wander too much she sat in the moment and finally responded to her father.

"Yes daddy, I'd love to join you on the golf course today. But not before I go on my walk for the day, any of you care to walk and talk?"

Minta touched George's hand and looked up at Scarlett, "I think you need go and have a little talk with Jesus, isn't that what the song says?"

"You're so funny but I think you're right mama. Daddy, when I come back, I'll get ready to go on the links with you."

"Alright baby, take your time and enjoy your walk."

CHAPTER 4

"It's starting to warm up pretty nice out there."

The breeze inside the club cooled everyone that walked inside, the humidity from the day was bringing in patrons left and right.

George pulled out a chair for Scarlett to be seated, "Here you go sweetheart, let's take a break and grab something to eat."

"So daddy, you brought your A-game today I see."

"Well you know, I've been at this for a while and now with all this free time on my hands, I'm getting better and better. I'm glad you decided to come with me."

After placing their drink orders, Scarlett acknowledged her dad, "I am too daddy. It was nice, the best part though was when those two cart jockeys ran into each other while texting on their phones."

George and Scarlett thought back to the thundering crash and at the same moment they both giggled aloud.

"Isn't it funny how they are supposed to be the ones managing the golf carts on the course and they couldn't even manage themselves."

"Sweetheart, that is too funny but you know what, sometimes we all need a little help managing ourselves. You know what I mean?"

Scarlett was about to respond when she heard in the not so far distance, "Hey George, how's it going?"

As George motioned for the friendly voice to come over, Scarlett turned around to see who would be coming their way. Who did she see? A tower of a man built with precision looking ultra-modern in his golf attire that transitioned well from the course to the club. His brilliantly bright smile caught her attention.

George stood to greet Dr. James Hartgrove, "Hello Dr. Hartgrove, how's that handicap of yours, is it getting any better?"

"I'm too embarrassed to even mention it, just know my handicap is handicapped. Hopefully one of these days when I grow up, I hope to be like you, George."

George patted Dr. Hartgrove on the shoulder, "You'll get there. Hey, I don't think you've had a chance to meet my daughter, let me introduce you two."

Standing to greet Dr. Hartgrove, he stopped her before she could get up, "Please no need to get up, I'm Dr. Hartgrove and it is a pleasure to finally meet you. Marilene, right?"

Extending her hand to shake the doctor's with a blush in her cheeks, she said, "Yes, I'm Marilene and it's nice to meet you as well."

Marilene was the name Scarlett had decided to go by for those who didn't know her. When she was younger, she had a doll by the name and had always loved the name. Using the name to craft a new identity seemed like a great idea.

Turning to George, "She's even more beautiful than you described sir."

Scarlett turned away to gather her thoughts for a quick moment, *"Has my daddy been talking to this man about me?"*

"Dr. Hartgrove, Marilene and I have only ordered drinks, do you have a table already, will you please join us?"

'I've told you before, please call me James and I think I'll take you up on your offer."

"Marilene, Dr. Hartgrove...I mean James here is a local cardiologist and he also lives here in the development, he's practically our neighbor."

"George, I guess if you consider living five miles apart neighbors then, yes, we're neighbors."

The impromptu trio laughed as the server brought over their drinks and took their food order.

James shifted from the casual table conversation to a more pointed dialogue with Scarlett.

"So, Marilene your dad here filled me in on some of the work you've been doing with your blog and the walking and talking program you've started."

Scarlett's skin bunched around her eyes as she settled on a pained stare at her dad, "Oh has he now? Dad?"

George dismissed Scarlett's blistering stare with a simple smile. He held up two fingers indicating a small portion and mouthed the words, "Only a little...just a little."

"Marilene, I think what you're doing is amazing and I'd like to talk to you more about it...in detail. I'm in the midst of planning a city-wide health fair and symposium and if you're interested, I'd love for you to be a part. As a doctor, I'm always looking for ways to get people motivated, ways to get them moving and it seems what you're doing is exactly what I need."

Scarlett felt her insides quivering, she started thinking of every worst-case scenario possible. She stroked her asymmetrical bob as a soothing gesture to calm herself.

James took a quick glance at his phone and blew out a sigh, "My apologies, there is an emergency at my office, I hate to leave in the middle of our lunch. But, I really need to go. Do you think I can call you later to discuss the event?"

Searching for the right words to say, Scarlett took a bite of her turkey club sandwich as James was gathering his things to leave.

George answered for her, "Yes, please call her to discuss...here is her number."

Scarlett now needed a gulp of water to wash down her sandwich and her pride that her father was rapidly destroying.

"Yes, that's fine Dr. Hartgrove and thanks to my father, you now have my number."

"Great, and please call me James. It's been my absolute pleasure meeting you, I'm sorry I have to leave but George, this one is on me. I'll have the server put lunch on my account. See you next time."

Before the doctor was even out of sight Scarlett blasted George, "What do you think you're doing? Why did you do that? There's no way I can be a part of his 'lil health care thingy. I'm supposed to be anonymous, remember? I've been trying this whole hiding in plain sight deal but c'mon dad. Apparently you've forgotten some very important details of my life."

George's softened features implied his calmness, he was unmoved by Scarlett's rant. Taking a deep, satisfying breath, "Sweetie, you have nothing to worry about. He has no idea about your situation. I think this is a great opportunity for your website and your program. More and more people are getting inspired to do something about their health because of your site, just by walking and talking. I truly believe James' health fair will provide you with greater exposure. It's not a big deal, we can hire a spokesperson, someone to be the face of it all, that way you can still stay behind the scenes."

No longer eating or drinking, Scarlett didn't know what to think. On one hand her dad was right. On her walk earlier that day, she felt as if she'd heard the Lord whisper to her the scriptures, 1 Timothy 4:11-16, she believed He was telling her to step up and use the gifts He'd placed within her and her writing was truly a gift and interestingly enough people were being blessed by it. Maybe the situation with Carson was a blessing in disguise and did have purpose. On the other hand, she couldn't afford for anyone to know who she really was, to discover her identity.

More than that, she had not had any thoughts about a man since leaving Carson, yet seated in the presence of Dr. Hartgrove, he caused her nerve endings to stir and tingle.

"Has your daddy ever steered you wrong...well let's not count the time I told you to wear that dress to your Junior Prom."

Both George and Scarlett thought back on the dress and at the same time they both let out a small shriek as they both shook just thinking about the dress.

"Okay, besides that dress, have I ever steered you in the wrong direction?"

"No, you haven't daddy."

"Alright then, trust your dad on this one, okay. I see nothing but good things here. All this anxiety you're working yourself into isn't worth it. Not for you or the baby. I have seen you go through so many changes with this ordeal but as your daddy, I want to tell you, it's time for you to humble yourself under the mighty hand of God. In due time honey, He's going to lift you up. The bible tells us to cast all our anxiety and cares upon Him, because He cares. Do you believe He cares for you sweetheart? Do you believe I care for you?"

Shielding her face with the napkin to conceal her tears, Scarlett dried her face and nodded in agreement towards her dad, "Yes and yes, daddy...I do believe."

CHAPTER 5

"Hello there husband."

"Well hello there wife."

Waking up from a nap, Carson rolled over to Rebekkah and kissed her passionately.

"I'm still getting a kick out of calling you my husband. I'm so happy to finally be Mrs. Carson Montgomery. Hey, it's the last day of our honeymoon on this beautiful island and we're choosing to spend it in bed? Who does that?"

Tickling his new bride under the covers Carson replied, "We do, that's who. Don't worry, your hubby has something planned for our last night. Our farewell dinner tonight is going to be awesome, you'll see."

"Well, it better be, especially after you promised me a two-month honeymoon and instead, we barely got a week together."

"Well after Bishop made his grand announcement at the reception, things had to change. We've had a great time this week together, haven't we?"

"Oh, you mean the reception we missed?"

Carson dismissed Rebekkah's whines about the honeymoon and the reception. Planting more and more kisses on her, Carson mentioned, "Just so you know, we'll be leaving quite early in the morning. Tomorrow is your first day at the church in your official capacity as my First Lady. Everyone now knows Bishop will be retiring and passing the baton over to me. So, you and I will need to be on point. I don't need any mishaps between now and then. Your stylist has already chosen three looks for you so you'll need to decide on one once we arrive. After that, you'll meet with my mother to go over any last minute details before service."

"Really? Honey, I understand all of that but do we have to talk about it now? Let's not talk about the church when we are here on our honeymoon. For goodness sakes, I mean how hard can it be? It's church. I'll be ready."

"Hey, you listen to me. You should always be ready to talk about this, this is now your life. This is my heritage, my livelihood...you just aren't going to be privy to the expensive cars, swanky houses, and fancy wardrobe without knowing what's going on at Wondrous Works. You better always be prepared to talk about this life. I'm telling you Rebekkah, I've been waiting on this for a long time and the time is finally arriving. Do you know how many women would love to be in your position? I chose you because you said you were down for me, Team Carson. Are you still down for Team Carson or is it now Team Rebekkah? Which is it, huh?"

Hesitating slightly and through clinched teeth, she responded, "Team Carson."

"That's more like it. Rebekkah, I don't need anything messing this up for me and I hope you understand your place in all of this. In case you don't, it's by my side...you are here to help make me look good. Pastoral."

Rebekkah's once relaxed body was now rigid and icy towards her husband, throwing back the covers to get up she said, "Fine. Alright, alright...I get it. I'm going to go take a shower now if you don't mind."

Actually, he did mind the shower. Carson pulled her back into the undefiled bed amorously and with intense fervor. Suspending his spirituality for a moment, he yielded to his carnality to satisfy his insatiable appetite.

CHAPTER 6

"Good evening, may I speak with Marilene?"

"Hello there Dr...I mean, James, this is Marilene. How are you tonight?"

"I'm fine, I hope I haven't called you too late? I just got in from a long day at my office."

"No, you're fine."

"Excellent, so how was the rest of your day? I hope you and your dad enjoyed your lunch. I hated that I had to leave, but duty calls right?"

"Absolutely. We actually ended up having a nice time together."

The flow of the conversation was going well and after a little more chit-chat, James dove right in.

"So, Marilene, I'd like to hear more about this program you've started."

Repositioning herself in the bed in an effort to feel comfortable so her nervousness wouldn't be heard over the phone, Scarlett took a deep breath and started at the beginning.

"Well, this past year has not been the best for me and I found myself questioning a lot of things that was supposed to matter, my life, my faith, my family. I came to my parents for what was supposed to be a week-long visit that has turned into about a six-month detour."

James was already intrigued by Scarlett's opening, he wanted to know more; he felt like he needed to know more.

"Every time I try to leave the nest...again, my parents place me on this humungous guilt trip that seems to be never ending. I know why they want me here but it still seems a bit ridiculous for me to be here."

"Wow, isn't it funny how life throws you these curve balls? I must say though; you appear to be handling whatever is going on with such grace. I'm sorry, I didn't mean to interrupt, please keep going."

"Why thank you. I can tell you this, it doesn't feel like it but that's how all of this kind of got started."

Sensing a certain openness, Scarlett began to speak freely.

"I found myself trying to pick up the pieces of my life and my parents kept trying to tell me to put my trust in God and that everything was going to be alright. All of that sounds good in theory but how do you actually put your trust in God when life is happening all around you?"

"You know, you're right...it can be hard when you're right in the middle of it."

"Exactly. At the time, I couldn't see how and honestly, sometimes, I still don't see it. Anyway, one day I felt the inclination to go for a walk and on my walk I just started going off on God. I mean, I was letting Him have it. I was telling Him how unfair I thought this situation was. Since my parents were telling me to depend on Him, I began to ask Him how am I do to that in this situation, how? Even with having my parents here, there were times I felt all alone. I went through some very dark days but little by little, I'd hear little things or look up and see signs that seemed to speak directly to my situation. If you can believe this, one day, a lady walked up to me, I didn't know her from Adam and she smiled and said, "Baby, be encouraged, all is well."

"Marilene, what an amazing story. So what happened after that?"

Reciprocating his intrigue with more information, Scarlett continued, "After one of those walks, I sat down at my computer and I began to write. I didn't have time to go and buy a journal because I was bubbling over with thoughts that I desperately needed to get out of me. My mother suggested I start a blog to document my walks and talks with Jesus and so I did. I quickly learned on those walks that when you walk with Christ, you'll never walk alone. What ended up happening was shortly after that my parents started walking with me and we'd talk while we were out. My dad started commenting on how he was sleeping better at night and my mother was sharing how she was losing a few pounds and inches as a result of the walks and I was blogging about all of this. Funny thing is, people starting finding my blog and started commenting about how they started walking and talking with their family members and the impact it was having on their lives. It's all still quite new, the blog is only like six months old but it is doing great which led me to actually create the 'Walking and Talking' program. And there you have it, that's my story and I'm sticking with it."

"Marilene, I couldn't be more impressed by you. I think you are just what the doctor ordered. As I mentioned earlier, I'm hosting a health fair in a few months and I think showcasing your program would be a wonderful addition. It seems to be a very simple approach to fitness that's getting people moving and with results. As a cardiologist, I'm all about getting people moving and those hearts pumping. I'm very passionate about heart health, now more than ever. Do you think you'd be interested in discussing this more, perhaps over dinner?"

Scarlett felt a strong desire to avoid a one-on-one meeting with James but she pushed passed it, "Sure, I talked it over with my dad and he thinks it's a great idea."

"See there, I knew there was a reason I liked George. Well, how about Monday evening?"

"Um, I have a late afternoon doctor's appointment on Monday so I'd rather not schedule a meeting for then."

"Oh, a doctor's appointment, is everything okay...is there anything I can help you with?"

"Uh, no you can't help me with this one doc, it's just a routine check-up, it's all good."

"Okay, well how about the next night? We both live here in the same neighborhood so we can meet back up at the country club if you like or we can go somewhere else, it's totally up to you."

"The club will be fine on Tuesday evening."

"Great, I'll make the reservations. It has been a blessing talking with you tonight, you actually said some things I needed to hear based on some things I've been going through, I may need to start walking and talking to

God myself. Ms. Marilene, I look forward to seeing you soon and I wish for you a good night."

"Good night James."

CHAPTER 7

"Boy, do I need some rest." Bishop Carson Montgomery plopped down on the bed fully dressed still wearing his hard-bottomed winged tips.

"Everything alright at the church honey?"

Regina was propped up in the lavish king-sized bed with several goose-down feathered pillows, she was reading her bible while talking to the Bishop.

"Yes, Regina. For whatever reason, I couldn't seem to get settled here in the study so I decided to go up to the church and prepare for my sermon tomorrow morning."

"Are you worried that Carson and Rebekkah won't make it back on time? Have you talked with him at all?"

Unloosening the grip on his paisley printed necktie and unbuttoning his French-cuffed shirt, Bishop's brain scrambled to find a logical reason to satisfy his wife.

"I can't really say what the issue was and no, I haven't spoken with that boy."

Regina placed her bible in her lap and proceeded to grant her husband a sidelong stare.

"It's her isn't it? You're distracted because of Delores, aren't you? You're not the only one who gets information around here. I heard that her husband died last week and that his funeral was today. That's what has you all distracted, isn't it? You should just go ahead and admit it."

"Regina, I can see that you're trying to start something with me and I'm too tired to even entertain your crazy questions. I'm going to go to bed and get me some rest so I can preach in the morning."

Bishop kissed Regina on her cheek and walked into the bathroom.

Delores Bolton, the heartbeat of C.E. Montgomery, III was unfortunately not born with the ministerial bloodline Carson Montgomery, II and his wife, Betty deemed appropriate for their son.

Delores and her family were members of Wondrous Works Tabernacle Fellowship when she and C.E. met and fell in love. Under his father's administration, C.E. and Delores kept their relationship hidden for years.

At the time, Delores and her family were grape pickers in the old wine country, they barely made enough to get by. Times were hard but through the help of the Lord, they always felt they had what they needed.

When C.E. decided he was going to propose and pledge his love to Delores after he graduated from Seminary, his plans were thwarted by the church administrator. Unbeknownst to him, the church administrator had taken notice to his spending while away at school, how he was sending money and expensive gifts to Delores. At the time she noticed the entry for the engagement ring, she brought the purchases to his parents' attention.

The slope of their noses were not long enough for how they looked down upon Delores when they summoned her to a meeting. They queried her on her family life, their financial situation, and her plans for the future. Seated in the church offices, upon learning Delores' mother had been bitten by a poisonous snake in the vineyards and the family was having a hard time paying for her medical bills and medication they informed Delores how they would offer her a well-paid position at the church and cover the medical expenses. The one condition. She would need to end her relationship with their son, Carson Eugene Montgomery, III.

Rightfully so, Carson was devastated. When he returned home after graduation, he lashed out at everyone around him. He couldn't understand his dear sweet Delores' decision to end things, nothing she said made sense to him.

How on earth did they expect him to work at the church alongside the love of his life and not be with her? One day the frustration mounted up so high, he exploded by turning over the desk where Delores sat and kicked a gigantic sized hole in the back.

He would never know the pain and anguish Delores would feel seeing her one true love suffer from the decision she made to help save her mother.

He had a hard time letting go, he tried to fight for Delores, even going up against his parents, letting them know he was going to marry her despite their disapproval. It didn't matter, Delores' mother was recovering and the Montgomery's were keeping their end of the deal which meant Delores had to keep hers.

Seeing their son spiraling out of control, with his passions raging like a mad man, they figured the best way for him to get over Delores was to introduce him to a well-respected, properly pedigreed young lady, none other than the radiant, Regina Van Pelt. Their preferred choice. She was the youngest daughter of Dr. R.J. Van Pelt, the presiding Bishop over the denomination to which hundreds of churches belonged, including Wondrous Works.

A six-week courtship proved long enough time for Regina and C.E., they married two weeks later.

Over time, C.E. and Delores found a way to work together but it was quite difficult. C.E. was devoted to Regina, he vowed to himself never stray away from his marriage but he found it hard to stop loving Delores. Unfortunately, it wasn't a button he could turn off at will. It doesn't work like that and whoever thinks it does is sadly mistaken.

If anyone ever saw C.E. and Delores together, the emotional connection they shared was purely undeniable...even to Regina who tried to turn a blind eye.

Around the age of five, Carson the fourth happened to be playing outside of his father's office when his ball bounced inside. The young Carson ran to retrieve the ball and he walked in on two people scared by love, longing for a different outcome, consoling each other in an intimate embrace. Their attraction was magnetic, in a way, they felt spiritually connected.

He picked up his ball, stood, and watched for a minute longer until the ball fell out of his hands and bounced on the floor towards his father's desk. The bouncing ball alerted C.E. and Delores to the little boy's presence. Despite nothing really happening between them, in horror, they wondered how long he had been there watching them.

Delores decided that night she could no longer work at the church. It had been years and yet, she and C.E. still shared deep feelings for one another. Nevertheless, he was happily married with children, their time together had come and gone.

The following week, she left town and never looked back.

As the moist steam filled the bathroom turning it into a sauna, Bishop sat on the toilet with his head in his hands. The truth of the matter was, Regina was right, he was thinking about Delores and how she must've been handling the death of her husband.

While at the church, he'd gone on her social networking pages to see comments and pictures from the day's funeral service. He couldn't resist, he sent her a private message expressing his condolence, letting her know he was praying for her.

Stepping into the marbled shower, he grabbed his chest, even after so many years, he realized he still had a prick in his heart for Delores. His heart was bleeding for the heartache she must've been going through now as a widow. His sympathy was sincere, he uttered another quick prayer for her and her family.

In the bedroom, hearing the shower running, Regina quickly grabbed her laptop and searched for Delores' online profile. Regina's timing was spot on. Minutes earlier, Delores had made a post:

> *"Thanks to everyone that has been so supportive to me and my family during our*

*time of bereavement. We appreciate every
act of kindness shown towards us. We know
Charles is now in the arms of Jesus and for
that, we are comforted.*

*I especially want to thank an old friend who
reached out to me tonight, it truly meant a
lot to me."*

Regina looked around some more and her mind
began to wander, *"Uh-huh, an old friend, huh? I
wonder if she's actually talking about my husband.
Yeah, right. I just bet it did mean a lot to you."*

Feeling her blood-pressure rising at a steady rate,
Regina placed her computer on the night stand and
turned off the lamp near her bed. She pretended to be
asleep when Bishop came to bed.

CHAPTER 8

"Here goes nothing." The contact sounds of snake-skinned stilettos onto the tiled floors pounded towards Regina's office door. The clicks of the heels were coming from the newly-wedded Mrs. Rebekkah Montgomery and she was on a mission. She eagerly knocked on the door but didn't wait for an acknowledgement.

Walking right into Regina's office with outstretched arms towards her new mother-in-law, Rebekkah greeted Regina, "Mama Montgomery, how nice to see you again."

Regina's body was stiff as a board, while Rebekkah's arms enveloped the matriarch of the Montgomery family, Regina's arms were flat, down by her side.

"Let's get something clear right off the bat. Mama Montgomery is not a name you will call me. That name was reserved for my daughter-in-love, Scarlett...Carson's first wife. You, my dear, will address me as First Lady."

Rebekkah's nostrils flared and her face reddened at the boundary lines Regina was drawing for her. She pressed her lips together to keep her hurt feelings from coming out by saying the wrong words.

Regina stood, offering a full-length inspection while Rebekkah took a seat on the sofa in the lounging area within Regina's office.

"Out of all the items your stylist chose for you today, that's what you decided to wear?"

Maintaining an even tone and presenting a phony smile, Rebekkah smoothed down her suit jacket, "Yes ma'am, this is what I chose. I think its conservative enough with a flair of femininity. Not to mention, my husband loved me in and out of it and gave me his stamp of approval."

Of the choices presented to her, Rebekkah chose a camel colored belted, jacketed sheath dress combination boasting classic lines with the jacket as it flourished with sweetness across the sweetheart neckline on the dress. Sweetheart necklines were a favorite of Rebekkah's.

Turning her back towards Rebekkah to grab a bottle of water, unmoved by her words, she suggested, "Let's go over the calendar...shall we?"

Pulling out her new personalized tablet Carson bought her as a wedding gift, Rebekkah answered, "We shall. Well, before we get started, I want to get on the calendar that next month, my family is throwing a baby shower for my sister. I've been very much involved in the planning and this will be the first time since Carson and I have been married that I'll get to see them."

Regina's arrogant laugh caught Rebekkah by surprise.

"Did I say something funny, First Lady?"

"Oh dear heart, unfortunately, all of your hard work planning your sister's shower will have to be enjoyed by everyone else who will attend."

"I don't understand what you mean."

"Well then let me make it real clear to you. Any and all Wondrous Works events take precedence over all others, personal or otherwise."

"And?"

"On the date of your sister's shower, you and I will be hosting my annual First Ladies luncheon at my home. This is something I started when Scarlett became part of the family. I'm very much a believer in Titus 2:4."[3]

"I still don't understand what this has to do with me. If this is something you and your beloved Scarlett started, why do I have to be there?"

"As the new wife of my son, you are sanctioned to be at all Wondrous Works events and this is one of them. I represent the older woman and you represent the younger generation. This is now an annual event and ladies from all over will be attending...including you."

Instead of smoothing the suit jacket, Rebekkah was now violently rolling her shoulders as if the once comfortable top was causing her some discomfort.

"I guess we need to go ahead and get this out in the open so do you mind if I ask you a question First Lady? You keep bringing up Scarlett's name and throwing her up in my face, but do you realize she left Carson and Wondrous Works high and dry...without a trace?"

"You can ask me one if I can ask you one. How do you think she must've felt when you were throwing it up in her face that you were sleeping with her husband? Oh yeah, you and Carson tried to play it off but, guess what, a wife knows, trust me on that."

---

[3] **Titus 2:4**: *"These older women must train the younger women to love their husbands and their children."*

Regina stepped into unchartered territory with Rebekkah. Regina had never once spoken of the secret infidelity to anyone yet she was full aware of it.

"I have no idea why Scarlett left the way she did but all I can say is, she must have had a heck of a reason for doing so. I miss her dearly. I pray for her daily and I hope she finds what she needs that she didn't feel she could get from here. From now on, when you approach me or talk to me about anything, you keep that little nugget in the front of your mind. If I knew about you two, I guarantee, she knew."

The revelation caught her off guard. With wet eyes, Rebekkah's tailor-fitted dress suit now seemed to fit too snug as she pulled and tugged at it to make herself less visible to her mother-in-law's scorn.

"I can only imagine what that poor girl must be going through. I want you to sit in that for a moment. Think of how she must be feeling. The pain, the betrayal, the constant stings of a failed marriage. Sit in it, I want you to feel it."

The knock at the door saved them both.

The voice on the other side shouted, "Five minutes until service, it's time to go in. It's show time."

Regina grabbed her belongings and prepared to walk out of the door, "Let this be the first lesson I teach you. Don't come for me or anyone else for that fact if you aren't ready to receive what they might have to give you. Don't you ever challenge me again; you hear me? Now get yourself together and let's go inside. This is what you wanted, right? You wanted the part, now you have it, so it's time to play it to the hilt. You may as well get over yourself, put your big girl panties on, and go praise the Lord."

CHAPTER 9

"And the countdown begins, we are starting in 5, 4, 3, 2, 1", shouted the stage manager.

Live in front of thousands and streaming before hundreds, the flashing lights, amazing media sets, the worship team, the dancers, the band, the congregation was highly exuberant for the Sunday morning worship service at Wondrous Works Tabernacle Fellowship.

Wondrous Works Tabernacle had been rooted and grounded in traditionalism but over the years the constitution of the ministry was now more contemporary with elements of tradition intertwined. Interestingly enough, the traditional structure of the ministry was actually appealing to the majority of their members.

The anointed praise and worship stirred the hearts of the people and prepared them for the message that would be preached by Bishop Montgomery.

The full production team of the ministry kept things rolling, without missing any cues. Everything was working according to schedule and as it should...except Rebekkah.

"Good morning, good morning to each and everyone one of you," the Bishop Montgomery greeted his congregants, "I'm so delighted you've chosen to worship with us today. We know you could've chosen to go anywhere but you decided to share your Sunday with us here at Wondrous Works. Well, I believe I have a word from the Lord for you today."

He turned to acknowledge his family that lined the platform on which he stood. The high definition cameras captured every angle of him and the entire sanctuary.

"So before I begin, I have to ask you to help me honor the First Lady, my First Lady...First Lady Regina, she looks so beautiful today. Without her, I don't know where I'd be. We honor you today honey."

Regina stood and greeted the audience with a blow of a kiss to her husband and a spirited wave to the crowd.

"Now, it gives me great pleasure to honor my son, Pastor Carson and his new lovely bride, Rebekkah. They flew in this morning from their honeymoon and we are so thankful they are home safe and sound."

The honors being bestowed upon Rebekkah was not breaking through to her, when Carson stood thinking she was going to stand with him, she was still seated. He quickly grabbed her by the arm to assist her to stand by him as they greeted the members of the church.

Fortunately, she was able to snap out of the trance and play the role but not without the other family members paying attention, including Regina.

"Our middle son Christian is now engaged, he and Courtney will be getting married soon and we are so happy for them. Can you all help me bless them today? God is doing some amazing things and we are so grateful."

Christian and Courtney stood and greeted their full-sized flock and then took their seats.

"I ask that you all keep praying for our youngest son, Cayden-James. We know God is in control and we believe God to do a wondrous work in him. Now, let's go to the word of the Lord. Let us pray."

Looking over his sermon notes one last time, Bishop began, "Today, I want to focus on a very familiar passage. Some of you can probably quote it faster than a knife fight in a phone booth. Some of y'all will get that on the way home. But, moving right along, let's go to the text. Turn with me to **Psalms 37:4** – "Delight yourself also in the Lord and He shall give you the desires of your heart."

"I'm guilty of this and I'm certain some of you are as well, quoting this when we want God to do something for us, like writing out a Christmas wish list to Santa Claus. But, I have a question for each one of us in here today and those of you who are watching. What sorts of things is your heart desiring?"

Subconsciously people nodded their heads as they pondered the question from their shepherd.

"The bible says in Jeremiah that the human heart is the most deceitful of all things. It says it's desperately wicked. Then it asks the question, who really knows how bad it is? There are countless scriptures that warn us about this 'ole heart of ours."

Bishop began to walk the parishioners through his message, breaking down certain meanings and intricate details of the text.

"When you hear the word desire, what things start to pop into your mind? Hey, hey, hey keep in mind, you're in the church house. Nah, seriously see the thing is, desire by itself is neither good nor bad. It is how you respond to those desires is where some people start having problems. Am I right about it?   In Genesis chapter four the Lord is talking to Cain, He says, "You will be accepted if you respond in the right way. But if you refuse to respond correctly, then watch out! Sin is waiting to attack and destroy you, and you must subdue it. I'm telling you, it's all in your reaction."

Having taken his time to properly lay the foundation, Bishop started finding his stride and picked up the pace.

"Going back to the fourth verse of Psalms 37, let's look at the word delight. The Strong's Concordance translates this word as 'anag', listen here, all you husbands in the house, just keep looking forward. Wives, I promise they aren't looking. You all do realize it is okay to laugh and have a good time in the house of the Lord? Amen. Seriously though, one way it's defined is to be happy about, to take exquisite joy."

Taking complete ownership of his platform and pulpit, Bishop posed another question, "How do you suppose we are to take delight in the Lord as David is admonishing us to? Well, if we are to have exquisite joy then we should be enjoying His presence, His company, and His will. Let me ask you this, how do you enjoy someone...you spend time with them, right? And guess what folks, when we take exquisite joy and delight ourselves in the Lord, we create synergy, we formulate an alliance. His desires become ours. As a result, we start seeing our prayers answered because now we're doing His will. I'm questioning y'all because I want you to really think about this thing. Take a quick minute and think about some desires you currently have in your heart; do they match up to what God wants? Are you seeking selfish gain or seeking how you can be a blessing to someone else?"

Carson's stomach began to feel hard, uncharacteristically, his nose started to run during the service and his eyes felt gritty. The words spoken by his father were having an impact on him, the questions caused his body to respond in a way that matched the mental responses he was having, as he mulled over his misdeeds with Scarlett.

Revving up for the close, he gave them the litmus test, "The way to determine if they match up is to figure out if it's God's will or my will. Our whole Christian existence is based upon abandoning our own will and following His. Sometimes that proves to be a struggle in life but that is what we should strive toward. I'm here to tell you, even as your pastor, I have to check my heart all the time. Uh, hello? Do you think because I stand behind this sacred lectern that I don't go through things? It's true, your pastor is human and I make mistakes too. None of us have it all together but that's the beauty about God because we don't have to. The more we don't have it together gives Him more room to work within us when we accept His way. I see, y'all don't believe me, well I'll give you an example and then I'll close. David did all sorts of things, he was a voyeur, he committed adultery and then orchestrated a murderous plot, among other things, yet, he wore the badge of being a man after God's own heart."[4]

"David succeeded the throne from his father-in-law, Saul. A stark difference in leadership styles...to say the least. But here is the thing I want you to get right here. The greatest difference between the two. Saul forgot about the will of God in search of securing his own will. The proof is found in 1 Samuel 13:13-14."[5]

Bishop continued on for a few more minutes and then closed out his message where they opened up the altar for altar call service.

"Listen to me church, the way we ensure we are reacting the right way to our desires is to desire a heart like the Lord's, I promise you this type of an exchange will never fail you. Will there be one today who will desire to have a heart like the Lord? If there will be one, come now."

He had preached out of his soul, he had great demonstrative aids, media clips, and funny stories. The countdown was on, by this time, everyone knew he would be retiring soon and he'd decided to give it all he had. He was determined to preach his best sermons yet during his remaining months as the head pastor.

---

[4] **Acts 13:22**: "And when He had removed him, He raised up for them David as king, to whom also He gave testimony and said, I have found David the son of Jesse, a man after My own heart, who will do all My will."

[5] **1 Samuel 13:13-14**: *And Samuel said to Saul, "You have done foolishly. You have not kept the commandment of the Lord your God, which He commanded you. For now the Lord would have established your kingdom over Israel forever. 14 But now your kingdom shall not continue. The Lord has sought for Himself a man after His own heart, and the Lord has commanded him to be commander over His people, because you have not kept what the Lord commanded you."*

The word for the day had touched everyone in the Montgomery family, all in different ways.

Based upon the line that snaked down the hallway from the bookstore and the audio and video sales for that day, the message also blessed the hearts of many who were in attendance. Their spiritual cups were filled, overflowing in some respects. They had enough to feast on until the next service time, the midweek service.

CHAPTER 10

Blazing past the dining room and slamming his suit jacket onto the island in the middle of the kitchen, the fruit bowl crashed to the floor from Carson's fury.

"Please tell me what in God's name is your problem? Are you still upset about the reception? Cutting the honeymoon short? I mean, are you trying to punish me for those things? You'd have to be because I can't figure out for the life of me why you would embarrass me and not to mention yourself during your first service as my wife."

Carson was all over the place, talking with his hands and pacing their kitchen floor in short spans, he was vexed by Rebekkah's debut at church. Barely giving her a chance to answer his barrage of questions, he continued to carry on and on.

"Father, God in Heaven, what have I done?"

Skipping the weekly, after church Sunday dinner with the family, Carson needed to talk to his wife, to get to the bottom of what happened with her.

"What do you mean, what have you done? Have you done something I don't know about Carson?"

"Hey, we're not talking about me right now. Forget about what I said. I want to know what happened to you up there today. I told you we can't afford for anything to go wrong. You should have known you were going to be scrutinized. Good gracious of life, you were fine when we got to the church, I actually thought you were excited about today's service. When I saw you walk out with my mother you looked like you had been hit by a bus."

Seated at one of the barstools, Rebekkah's slumped shoulders rested on their textured, concrete countertops, "You're exactly right because that's about how I felt after the meeting I had with your mother."

"I need to hear what on earth she could have said to make you look like that?"

Rebekkah's head tipped back on her neck, allowing her to look at the skylight in their ceiling.

"Okay, so let's start with how I'm to address her. She shot me down trying to call her Mama Montgomery. In no uncertain terms she let it be known that I was to address her as the First Lady."

"Are you kidding me, are you serious right now? Her saying that to you has you this bent out of shape?"

"Oh no, it wasn't just that. I don't know, maybe it was her crushing my plans to attend my sister's shower that I've worked so hard on. Since every detail of our wedding was planned out, I was glad to be able to plan her shower."

Not yet understanding, with his hand on his waist, "Okay, so you won't make the shower. I'm sure your sister will understand you can't make it. Is that what caused you to check out?"

"I'm not done, there's more. It could be the fact she made it a point to remind me that I'm not her darling Scarlett."

"Scarlett? What did mama say about her? So what Rebekkah, that is something you might have to get used to. Scarlett was my wife for almost six years and people did love her. You may encounter some of that around here. None of that still seems to measure up to your behavior. If you can't handle a little tough meeting with my mama, I just -."

Rebekkah retreated inward and yelled out, "She knows Carson."

"Knows what? Honey, you aren't making any sense to me."

"She knows that you and I were having an affair while you were married to Scarlett and she made for darn sure to call me out on it. You happy now, am I making sense to you now?"

Carson's muscles jumped under his skin, he began to shake his head in denial.

"I don't know Carson, this already seems like it's too much, more than I bargained for. Sitting in the pews week after week, your mind starts to convince you that you can do a better job than the one currently in the position but...this is hard. People don't really know what goes on behind the scenes."

Carson walked over to Rebekkah, reached for her and pulled her down from the barstool where he held her close.

"Everything is going to be okay, things will get better. Team Carson, remember."

"When does Team Carson plan on talking to his mama?"

The hunger pains bouncing around Rebekkah's stomach called out into the open. She and Carson had not eaten since before boarding the jet before service.

"Honey, I think something else needs more attention, like your stomach, maybe? I'll even take you to your favorite restaurant. C'mon, let's go."

CHAPTER 11

"Oh Scarlett, it finally happened. My goodness, it's like your belly popped out overnight and it couldn't have happened on a better day."

Minta bounced from one foot to the other with her hands in the air while taking liberties to rub on Scarlett's enlarged stomach.

"Finally, the doctor will have some room to work with at your appointment today when we find out who you are carrying in there....is it a little prince or a princess."

"Mama, I'm going to need for you to calm down. The appointment isn't until later this afternoon and if you keep going like this, you're going to be too tired to go."

Minta was steadily moving about, unable to stay still. Cooking breakfast, dancing in the kitchen, smiling at Scarlett and then of course, smiling at her tummy.

"When I carried you and your brother, my body didn't give me a chance to pop out, seems like I ballooned as soon as I found out I was pregnant. I got big as a house, both times. Maybe because you have such a petite frame, whatever the case, I'm glad to see it."

"You're right though, it does seem like it just popped out."

Scarlett was now able to rub her stomach in circular motions, she sparkled like a treasure chest of jewels thinking of the tiny miracle she was chosen to carry.

"I'm starting to understand why you love me so much. I'm already in love with this little person that I don't even know. I'm so excited to find out the sex of my baby today. Any thoughts? Any bets?"

Minta's body was constantly in motion, she was moving about nonstop.

"I will wear the color of my prediction to the doctor's appointment so when we get ready to go, you'll know what I think."

Scarlett caught a case of the giggles. "You think daddy would be willing to do the same thing? He swears it's a girl but since he made fun of Cole last year for wearing a pink shirt, I wonder if he'd go through with it."

Scarlett checked the time on the stove, "Mama, he already left for his tee time, right? I think I'll text him and see what he says."

Within minutes the phone buzzed, Scarlett cackled.

Minta looked around at Scarlett. "Girl, what did your crazy daddy say?"

"He said, I'll do anything for my little princess. By the way, as Cole taught me, real men wear pink. Oh my goodness, this baby is driving y'all bananas."

Placing the phone back down on the table it vibrated again. "I wonder if daddy's changed his mind."

The buzz alert was not from her dad. James Hartgrove was texting.

"GM, thinking bout u 2day, hopin ur appt. goes well. Looking 4ward 2 biz dinner☺."

Scarlett read the message like twenty times in under one minute, she touched the phone ever so slightly thinking of how nice it was for him to remember her.

"What did George say this time?"

Tightly pressing her lips to keep from smiling, Scarlett answered her mother, "Actually, that wasn't daddy."

Minta's motions slowed a bit to take notice.

"Well, I ain't trying to be all up in your business but I see you over there trying to keep from smiling and your eyes are doing something a little different girly, so who's the message from?"

Pretending to laugh off her mother's comments, Scarlett shouted, "Mama!"

"What...I call it like I see it, so who was it? You know what, how about this, I don't need for you to tell me because I already know who it's from."

"So who is the message from mama?"

Minta spoke with full assurance in her voice, "The messenger my dear darling Scarlett is none other than that fine-looking Dr. James Hartgrove. Tell me I'm wrong."

"You're wrong. I'm lying...you're right."

"I know I'm right, George told me about the two of you having lunch with him at the club the other day. According to your father, Dr. Hartgrove seemed to be quite taken by you. George said he'd talked about you a couple of times during some of their golf games about your new program and the doctor mentioned how he would like to meet you to discuss it."

Pouring another glass of orange juice, Scarlett said, "I'm starting to feel a little set up here. Did daddy set me up by going to the golf course with him the other day because he knew that guy would be there?"

"I don't know about all of that. All I know is that he'd said to George on more than one occasion that he was interested in hearing more about you and your blog. Speaking of, we should go on our walk today before we leave for the appointment. Getting back on you, I tend to think it doesn't hurt that he's single. I'm mean, you're single, he's single."

Pushing her seat back to stand up erect and pointing wildly to her stomach.

"Earth to Minta, earth to Minta. I know you've noticed, shoot, everyone will be able to notice now, I'm PREGNANT...with another man's baby."

"Oh Scarlett, you have always been so dramatic. I'm going to say this to you and I mean it with everything in me...so what?"

"So what? Really mama, really?"

"Yes, really. Scarlett, yes you were hit with a serious blow, yes, I wanted to put my foot clean up Carson's, you-know-what but it's clear and evident to me God is doing something through you. The more you try and figure and work things out instead of surrendering to the process, you keep yourself stuck. You came here to start over, then do that, start over. When you embrace this time in your life and use it as an opportunity to get closer to God, you'll begin to see Him move in a mighty way."

Baring down on her teeth Scarlett knew Minta was right.

"Mama, I know all of what you are saying is right, I used to teach this same stuff in my young adult classes. Sometimes it's just hard to put things into perspective when you're actually living with a completely different outlook."

Taking Scarlett's hand in hers, "I know you are a teacher of the Word but I have to ask, are you a believer of it? Sweetie, I'm not saying that Dr. Hartgrove is the man for you, right now, I'm sure your focus is on the baby, as it should be. However, keep in mind, Carson has already remarried. There is no reason, you couldn't...even with a baby."

Scarlett's hands moved before her head could tell her to stop replying to the text: **"Ah, thx. C u 2moro nite.☺"**

CHAPTER 12

"Pastor Carson, Pastor Carson, hey, over here."

Carson searched out the voice calling out to him, he saw Maria Caldwell, a member of Wondrous Works.

Greeting Maria with great enthusiasm, "Well hello there Maria, how's it going today? How's the family?"

"Everyone is doing well, thanks for asking pastor. So what brings you into the bank today?"

"I'm glad you stopped me, you may be able to help me with something."

"Sure thing, let's walk over here to my office."

Inside of Maria's office, Carson was being very attentive towards her as she went on and on about her children, his smile and nods seemed to validate Maria, she talked and talked and then talked some more.

"Well, enough about me, how can I help you today?"

Scooting towards the edge of his seat and leaning forward in an effort to bring Maria into a tight knit group, he asked, "Is it possible for you to tell me where my ex-wife, Scarlett has been using her bank cards?"

"Are you still on her account?"

"No, I'm not. I was able to get removed, you know, when she left me."

"Oh yeah pastor, I'm so sorry about that, I was so heartbroken, I loved First Lady Scarlett but listen, better days are ahead. Congratulations by the way."

"Thanks so much, it's been hard but God has sustained me and sent me someone else. So, about her account."

"Yeah, unfortunately if you aren't on the account, I'm unable to share any information with you about it."

Carson flaunted his devilish smile that always seemed to put people at ease and win their trust and loyalty. *"I see I need to thaw her out a little bit, she seems to be one of those by-the-book types."*

"Are you sure there isn't anything you can do for your pastor, Sis. Maria?"

"I mean, I wish I could but if I did this, I could lose my job and I can't afford that being a single mother of four children."

Carson turned up the compassion on the empathetic meter, patting Maria on her hand.

"Your pastor would never want you to lose your job trying to help him out. This would just mean so much to me, I need to see if I can try and locate Scarlett. She made it perfectly clear when she left she didn't want to be found but I really need some closure. I need to know what mistakes I made with her so I don't subconsciously make them with my new wife. You understand don't you Maria?"

Maria rubbed at the middle of her forehead with her eyes closed thinking she was being confronted with a tough decision. What was a devoted church member to do?

"Indulge me for a minute. Let's just say that I pulled up a particular account and printed out certain information from said account. If I so happened to leave those printouts on my desk and then happened to walk out for a minute, there isn't anything I could do if your eyes just so happened to see the items on my desk...right?"

Carson squared his shoulders back, "I see what you mean." Continuing on with the scenario, "A person just might happen to glance at something on your desk by accident and you couldn't be held liable for that."

Maria pulled up Scarlett's account and printed out the bank card transactions. She plopped them down on her desk without looking at them and hurriedly walked out of her office without saying a word.

Looking over the documents, Carson thought, *"Hmmm, Scarlett's transaction history is blank, she's not using her bank card anywhere. Scarlett, where are you? I've tried looking up your family and nothing. Where are you girl?"*

Maria slowly walked back to her office praying no one saw her pastor looking at things on her desk.

Pastor Carson was gone.

CHAPTER 13

"Scarlett Watson."

Scarlett and her parents who were a half an hour early to her appointment walked out of the patient waiting area. George sported a pink polo shirt whereas Minta was adorned in a light blue sparkly top, and Scarlett was clothed in all white.

Inside of the examination room, Scarlett's doctor came in and greeted the trio.

"Good evening everybody, how's everyone doing today? I'm guessing by the color choices this is the family's predictions on the sex of the baby right?"

Everyone nodded in agreement.

"It doesn't matter to me; all I want is a healthy baby. I'm fine either way, doesn't matter to me whether we have lashes or mustaches, I'll be happy no matter what."

"Well Scarlett, I actually need to talk to you about that."

Minta didn't wait for Scarlett to respond, "Is everything alright doctor?"

"Scarlett, you had your blood screenings recently and we've reviewed the results and it appears that your baby is at an elevated risk of the genetic disorder we know as Down's Syndrome."

Unsure of what to ask, Scarlett still wanted to know about the sex of her baby, "Given this type of information, will we still be able to determine the sex today Dr. Johnson?"

"Absolutely. In fact, we brought in a sonographer who specializes in recognizing certain markers for determining genetic disorders. She will be in here shortly to see you."

When Dr. Johnson left the room, Minta grabbed both George's hand and her daughter's hand and went into prayer warrior mode:

> *"Father God, we come before you right now with humble hearts. Your word tells us that in all things, we are to give thanks and so Father, right now we thank You for this situation. We also know that where two or three are gathered together in your name, there You are in the midst and right now God, we need you in the midst of this information. Father, we know that this baby is fearfully and wonderfully made and that you don't make any mistakes. Father, the fruit of Scarlett's womb is blessed and we thank you Lord for that. You told us in Your word to come boldly before Your throne of grace, where we may obtain mercy and find grace to help us in our time of need. Strengthen Scarlett in her body and keep her mind, Lord. Grant us with Your grace,*

whatever the outcome is, we ask you to give us the grace to work out whatever the details are. We love you and we bless Your holy name. In Jesus name we pray. Amen."

Scarlett was teary-eyed, "I don't understand this; I don't understand what's going on."

George stepped up and place his hand on her shoulder. "Let's just see what the doctors come up with okay. It doesn't matter what they say, this is a blessed baby."

Jasmine, the sonographer walked into the room and greeted the family, "I see the gang's all here, huh? Normally, I'd ask for predictions but I can pretty much tell where everyone stands."

That joke usually worked but the tone in the room was stifling.

Noticing Scarlett's disposition, Jasmine touched Scarlett on her leg, "Are you going to be alright?"

"I'll be fine. I'm just trying to process this new information."

Not knowing exactly what to think and for fear of thinking the wrong thoughts towards the situation, Scarlett's mind froze out all incoming and outgoing thoughts, her mind was completely blank. The chill of her anxieties made her cool to the touch, she shivered unconsciously.

Watching every little detail, Minta asked, "Scarlett, are you cold? Do you need a blanket or a jacket?"

Jasmine and Minta unfolded a blanket onto a frigid Scarlett.

"Yeah, well about that and why I'm here. I'm going to get started on my examination. So, just so I'm clear, you do want to know the sex, right? I don't want to spill the beans if we are wanting to be surprised."

Inserting herself into the mix without permission, Minta blurted out, "Can you start the test already?"

A fifteen minute exploration seemed like a lifetime. Scarlett and her family watched with great intensity as Jasmine did the sonogram. Catching a couple of hand waves to the family and a few yawns captured the hearts of a proud mommy-to-be and future grandparents. They all were in awe of the miracle on the black and white screen.

During the examination, there was a knock at the door.

Jasmine hopped up, "Yes, hopefully, this is the information I was waiting on. Give me one quick second and I'll be right back."

Jasmine walked back in the room with a file in her hands and a smile that seemed to span for miles.

"I have good news and I have good news. Which would you like first?"

"Were you able to find anything?"

"The only thing I was able to find was that you are twenty-four weeks pregnant with a baby BOY."

Before George could get happy, he asked, "What about the other thing, the markers for the -."

Jasmine's smile interrupted him.

"That's the other good news I have. They brought me in today for your sonogram and when I got your file and looked it over, something was not sitting well with me. I looked and looked and looked until I found it. The lab where you had your blood screenings entered in the wrong date of birth for you and so it made it look like you were a woman over fifty trying to have a baby. In an instance such as this, your baby would be at an elevated risk of being born with a genetic disorder."

Minta confirmed, "So in other words?"

"So, in other words, I had the lab rerun the results with Scarlett's correct birthdate and the tests came back normal. Your baby is fine. Congratulations. I'll let the doctor know, I'm sure she'll be back in to speak with you."

Scarlett got up from the table and hugged Jasmine and with joyful tears flowing rapidly. She thanked her over and over again. "Thank you for having the presence of mind to check into it and not let up. I thank God for you."

Scarlett had a desire to do anything to repay Jasmine for her fortitude in her situation. "What's your favorite restaurant, favorite store, do you need anything, what can I do for you? Is there anything?"

Both George and Minta did the same, hugging and thanking Jasmine.

"Family, this is thanks enough, promise me when he's born, you'll send me a picture and spoil him rotten."

Jasmine made a dignified exit from the room. These were the moments she loved her job.

"A grandson." George stood in amazement. He pulled out a light blue polo and put it on. I only wore that shirt for y'all, I knew it was a boy all along."

In a dismissive way to George, Minta retorted, "Whatever. Yeah, I just bet you knew. You are something else. You handsome grandpa, you."

The atmosphere was much different than in the preceding moments.

"I already have a name picked out. I think he should be named...uh, yes, George."

"Daddy, you're a mess. I haven't even thought about names."

"Well, you have a couple of months left to decide. Oh my goodness, what a blessing. God is so good. Grandma Minta has already starting knitting for her new baby boy. I really knew it was a boy. You can look at her and tell how she's carrying that she's having a boy."

The playful banter between George and Minta continued on while Scarlett got lost in the moment. "*My parents are so happy about becoming grandparents while the Montgomery's have no idea about their grandson. Their son stole this moment from them. Carson may think he tried to break me by hatching this crazy plan but he has no idea he has given me the greatest gift and as long as I live, I'll protect my baby from ever coming in contact with him.*"

Scarlett looked down at her stomach and rubbed it from top to bottom as she mouthed, "I love you baby boy, it's just you and me kid."

George and Minta gathered Scarlett's things and helped her up, George kissed her on the cheek, "I'm so proud of you baby, I feel like celebrating. Dinner is on me tonight."

CHAPTER 14

"Hi Dr. Hartgrove, it's so nice to see you again."

"Hi there, how's our patient doing today?"

Dr. James Hartgrove had a reputation for his excellent bed side manner, he carried strong emotional connections with his patients.

"I'm doing much better, thanks to you. I really appreciate you taking the time to research and find the right medication that would work for me."

"Oh, that's wonderful news and it's my pleasure to be your physician. In that case Clara, I'm going to write you another script, I can send it directly to your pharmacy if you like. Is the pharmacy on record the one you want it sent to?"

The light-hearted exchange between Dr. Hartgrove and his patient took a sharp turn as he started filling in the tabs on the computer. In a quick glance in the bottom corner he noticed the date, his face and ink pin both dropped to the floor.

"Dr. Hartgrove, are you alright, is everything okay?"

The doctor briefly stood motionless, trying urgently to compose himself in front of Clara. He'd been moving all morning; he had not had a chance to give any thought to what the date was.

"Yes, Clara...thanks for asking but I'm fine. Your prescription has been filled. You take it easy and I'll see you next time at your monthly follow up visit."

Dr. Hartgrove tore down the hallway to get to his front desk staff, "Dr. Morris is already here but call in Dr. Collins to cover for me as well. Something has come up and I'll be taking off the rest of the day."

"Is everything alright doctor?"

"Yes, don't worry, just please do as I've asked and get Dr. Collins in right away, I've already spoken to Dr. Morris. If things get too crazy, you can call me but please try to manage without me today. I'll see you all tomorrow."

"Yes sir."

CHAPTER 15

"Hey Ms. Anita, it's me....James. I thought I'd call and check on you."

"Today has been a tough one for me but no matter what I'm still blessed by the best. How you doing son?"

"I was with a patient today and I happened to glance at the date on the computer and I nearly came undone...today would have been her thirtieth birthday."

"It's hard to believe she's already been gone a year, some days when I'm in here by myself it feels like it just happened yesterday. While I miss her dearly, I know she's in a better place."

Cheryl Adams and James had been dating off and on for three years while James tried to get his practice up and running. Once he was finally established in his career, he knew he was going to marry Cheryl. She had been loyal, patient, and supportive of everything he did. Although his time was always scarce, he supported her endeavors as an actress in the best ways he could.

"Yes, she is in a better place and because of her so am I. I've shared with you many times before but I'm so grateful because in her death, I learned about eternal life."

Growing up, James' family was not affiliated with any particular church, his parents were scientists and they held their own beliefs about a supreme being and how the world worked. Spirituality wasn't a big issue for them. His parents did however impart in him the importance of love and compassion at an early age.

"Boy, you should have seen how you were looking at all of us praying over Cheryl in that hospital."

"I remember it like it was yesterday, I felt like while I was busting my butt trying to find a solution to her heart problem and all y'all were doing was saying silly stuff over her. I really felt like y'all could have been doing more or something else more worthwhile. I would have done anything to save her, I would have gladly taken her place if I could have. I mean, I'm one of the top cardiologists around, I should have been able to do something for her."

Cheryl was hosting a softball tournament for her foundation when she collapsed onto the diamond. The crowd was horrified at the sight of the paramedics rushing to resuscitate Cheryl, including her beloved, James Hartgrove.

Cheryl was quickly rushed to the nearest hospital where the team of doctors concluded she'd suffered a stroke as a result of a congenital heart defect that was never detected.

With few breaths left in her limp body, she was supported by breathing machines. In those few days, James frantically searched for a solution to save Cheryl including fast tracking her on the heart transplant list.

The fateful day came when her mother, Anita decided to pull the plug, not that she wasn't believing for a miracle but she had accepted within her heart the inevitable.

"Ms. Anita, when I heard you say, "To be absent from the body means to be present with the Lord. I thought you had lost your ever loving mind. I had no idea what you were talking about."

"But I bet you know now, don't you son?"

James' eyes began to get full. "I sure do. In her death, I learned the meaning of eternal life in that crowded hospital room. To be a witness to her spirit leaving this world and entering into another, was a spiritual awakening for me. In that moment, nothing mattered to me. My money didn't matter, my credentials, my awards, none of that stuff. I found myself wanting to know more about God and what you meant about being present with the Lord. I did all I could to save her but she actually saved me. Through her, I found the true meaning of life."

"Son, I remember walking with you to the chapel where you accepted Jesus into your heart. It is truly a day; I'll never forget James. While I know she's with the Lord, there are some days I miss her so much. She was my only child. I miss seeing her beautiful smile but I know that I'll see her again one day."

Anita's sorrow became audible; she began to weep on the phone. Tears were already falling from James' face.

"You know what Ms. Anita; I have an idea. I don't think you should be alone tonight, how about you come over to my house for dinner? We can order some food and have a celebratory birthday dinner in Cheryl's honor. What do you think?"

"Now son, I wouldn't want to put you out or anything, Ms. Anita will be alright."

"Nonsense. I won't hear of it. That day in the chapel I adopted you as my spiritual mother. You are family to me, you could never put me out of anything. What would you like to eat tonight?"

"I don't know, how about you surprise me."

"I'll do just that. Should I come get you or should I send a car for you?"

"No need to trouble yourself, I can drive myself over there. What time should I come over?"

"Let's say, be here by seven o'clock."

James began making preparations for the impromptu birthday dinner for Cheryl, he figured, he'd order Cheryl's favorite, Thai food from her favorite restaurant when it hit him, *"Oh no, Marilene."*

CHAPTER 16

"You're going out on a date with James Hartgrove tonight, huh?"

"No, I'm going to meet James Hartgrove at the club for dinner to discuss the walking and talking campaign, daddy."

Scarlett sat down across from George in the sunroom where the natural light brightened the entire room.

Shrugging his shoulders, "Same difference to me. Coming to hang out with your old man?"

"I promise to God, you and mama are unbelievable. I'm not going on a date. When did two people having a business dinner become going on a date?"

George kept a steady eye on his newspaper and his daughter.

"Mere semantics, Scarlett. I think it's a good thing. I'm glad you're going to have a chance to get all dolled up and have some fun, business or otherwise."

"I said this to mama the other day but you guys seem to keep forgetting the fact I'm six months pregnant with another man's baby."

"A man who is no longer a part of your life...thank God. A man who never deserved you in the first place. I say good riddance to that thug in a preacher's suit. I haven't forgotten at all but what I have forgotten is Carson, what's his name?"

Scarlett's fingers spread out in a fan across her breastbone, "Well sir, well sir, why don't you just tell me how you really feel about it."

"I'm aggravated that you still spend any amount of brain cells thinking about that punk. A baby doesn't have to keep you from finding happiness with someone who will not only love you but also your son. I want you to keep that in mind Scarlett. I came across plenty of customers, single mothers at the bank who did not always stay single. You're a woman, you can't teach a boy how to be a man. Only a man can do that. Any man can make a baby but it takes a real man to be a father. Trust me, there are still some honorable men out there who believe in family."

Scarlett tilted her head to the side, did her dad have a point? *"Somehow, I can't help but wonder if anyone else would be interested in me with a child? Plus, with what happened in my marriage, relationships are overrated. My own husband didn't want me so how can I expect someone else to?"*

"Daddy, I don't need a man to fulfill me. The one I had didn't do it so why would I look to another one to fulfill me? Plus, I have you and Cole to teach my boy how to become a man."

"Believe that lie if you want to Scarlett but you're on your own with that."

The vibration from her phone broke her concentration. They were both grateful for the distraction.

"Is that James texting you to confirm for this evening honey?"

It was James but it wasn't a confirmation. The text read:

"Scarlett, please accept my sincerest apologies. Sum10 has come up and I need 2 resched our mtg 4 this eve. Call u 2moro."

Scarlett laid back on the sofa and propped her feet up, "I guess I will be hanging out with you, he has to reschedule. He says he'll call me tomorrow."

"Do I detect a bit of disappointment in your voice Ms. I don't need a man to fulfill me?"

Scarlett clasped her hands behind her head, "Of course not, it was just dinner, remember."

The false bravado was nice for George but deep down inside, Scarlett did find herself feeling some kind of way about James cancelling their dinner.

CHAPTER 17

"**G**ood morning Marilene, this is James...James Hartgrove. I hope I haven't called you too early this morning."

"Hey, how's it going? No, you're fine. I wake up early so I've been up for a while already."

"Well, I wanted to call and officially apologize for last night. My day took a completely different turn and due to unforeseen circumstances, I had to cancel or shall I say, reschedule."

"Oh, you're fine. I completely understand, things happen. I ended up going to the movies with my dad."

James had a slow smile that started to build, "So I was really hoping that you're free tonight and I was thinking that as a way to make it up to you that instead of going to the club, we could actually go out to another spot...you pick, my treat."

Scarlett's nervous laugh was amusing to James.

"Yes, tonight is fine. I'm free to go out tonight." Scarlett's throat felt as if it was growing a thick layer of glob, *"OMG, did I just say, I'm free to go out, like actually go out. Am I really going out tonight?"*

James' face beamed, "Perfect. So what's the rest of your day looking like?"

"Not too much, I was getting ready to go on my daily walk right before you called and after that my mother and I were planning to go shopping."

"Uh-huh, the infamous walk...are you walking with someone today?"

"No, I was going to go by myself this morning."

"Do you mind if I join you, can we walk and talk this morning?"

Scarlett's muscles twitched, she wasn't sure how to respond. *"I'm going to see him tonight; do I really want to see him twice in one day?"*

"Sure, you can come along. Don't you have a job to go to, what time do you have to be at work?"

"See that's one of the good things about being the boss and being in private practice, I get to enjoy the luxury of flexibility."

"Alright now, I hear you Dr. Hartgrove. So, I'll meet you up at the club, let's say in about thirty minutes and then we can walk from there. How does that sound?"

"Sounds like a plan, see you in a bit."

CHAPTER 18

"I love waking up to you Carson Montgomery. What was that commercial back in the day, the best part of waking up, is Carson in my arms...I think that's how it went."

"Well, we know you won't be using your gifts and talents on the praise and worship team girl."

"Oh hush up Carson, are you really going to make fun of my singing when I was trying to tell you how much I love you?"

"I can make fun of the singing because God didn't bless you with that talent but He sure blessed you with others, come here girl."

Carson touched and held Rebekkah close and she engaged him lovingly.

"See what I mean, who needs to sing when you can do things like that? Girl, God has blessed you with multiple talents. I could preach a sermon right there. Your gifts have surely made room for you...that was incredible. Praise the Lord."

Sitting up to a curtsy in the bed, "Rebekkah aims to please. Now that I'm your wife, it is my job to stay on top of my game and to make sure you enjoy the highest levels of satisfaction, satisfaction that only I can give. I plan to blow you away and pleasure you beyond your wildest dreams."

Using an apt dialogue to sum up his present situation, Carson screamed, "Glory."

Carson's blissful consciousness found him caressing Rebekkah's back in the afterglow of their love, not thinking clearly, he stepped off into enemy territory.

"Midweek service is tonight, are you going to be better prepared tonight than you were on Sunday?"

"Only if your monster of a mother stays out of my way, I'm not in any hurry to be around her in any way shape or form."

Slowly coming out of the blessedness of the morning's activities, Carson looked at Rebekkah and said, "Now Scarlett, you're being silly. You and my mother have to work together, there is no way of avoiding her."

Pulling back the covers of the bed towards her body and exposing Carson's, Rebekkah exchanged her once seductive voice with an indignant one, "What did you just call me?"

"Hey, what are you doing? Give me the cover back. I said, Rebekkah you're being silly. There's no way you can get around my mother. Isn't there a big planning meeting for that upcoming luncheon at her house?"

Carson's mouth had betrayed him and he was completely unaware of his infraction.

Tugging the covers back once again, "No, you did not say that you called me Scarlett."

"I did not, you're hearing things. Why would I call you Scarlett... that just doesn't make any good sense? She left me, remember? You and I are together now so what's your point?"

A flash of anger crossed Rebekkah's face as Carson mentioned Scarlett's name. "The point is that; I'm not going to live around here in the shadows of the ghost of Scarlett's past. I won't do it Carson. You, your mama, and everybody else better get used to having me around."

Carson wrapped the covers over his body one more time and stroked his wife's arm. "I love you Rebekkah Montgomery."

Rebekkah scoffed at Carson's confession, "Yeah but I'm starting to wonder do you still love your ex-wife? It's apparent to me now that everyone is comparing me to her and she's the one that left."

Carson turned away from Rebekkah where he became unnaturally quiet and still.

Rebekkah reached for her silky, crimson colored chemise and walked away from their bed.

"Oh and Carson, I'll be ready for tonight's service but I think you need to think about whether or not you are ready and prepared for us."

CHAPTER 19

"**I**'d better hurry up, I told James thirty minutes and here I am about to be late."

Scarlett drove her dad's personal golf cart up to the club. She parked and stood outside to wait for James to arrive.

Excited about having a walk and talk session with Scarlett, James hurried up to their clubhouse.

The spring morning air felt refreshing, it was a beautiful day as he scanned the landscape of the area. The magnolias were blossoming and the blooming dogwoods created an ornamental picture as they lined the curvy roads of the immediate area.

Arriving up at the pro shop, he spotted the back of Scarlett where he stood and admired her rear-view. Scarlett's smooth and rounded legs matched her rounded hips, he was enjoying the scene of Scarlett until he caught sight of her side profile, a rounded belly to match.

The unexpected observation stopped him midstride, "*Whoa, where did that come from? She's pregnant? How did I miss that?*"

Clearly caught off guard, James tried to determine his next move. He didn't want Marilene to see he was surprised by her impending bundle of joy.

He couldn't help but think back to the conversation he'd had the night before with Ms. Anita and how when he first saw Marilene standing at the club he thought the two were somehow connected.

He glanced over and noticed her checking the time on her watch, *"I don't want to keep her waiting any longer. Put your game face on James."* He whispered a quick prayer.

"Good morning, I see you're ready and waiting to walk and talk. Are you by chance waiting on me?"

James greeted her as if nothing was different or that a baby boy was standing in the middle of them.

"Why is he acting like he doesn't see that I'm pregnant?"

"Hi, yes I'm ready to walk and talk and I have been waiting on you."

"Well wait no more. I'm ready, let's walk. So Marilene, how far do you usually walk?"

"I try to get in at least thirty minutes of walking in but it all depends on who I'm walking with, if I'm by myself, and/or if the Lord begins to speak to me. Within the program I'm developing the idea is to try and accumulate at least ten thousand steps a day no matter how you get them. The other part is that within those ten thousand steps you should have you an accountability partner, someone who can help motivate and keep you accountable towards your progress, hence walking and talking."

"I love it. I'm completely sold on the idea and as far as I'm concerned, I want you and your program front and center at the health expo. I've already spoken to the organizers about this and they are excited about the concept and meeting you."

Scarlett stopped the high-speed stroll.

"About that. I'm a behind the scenes person, not front and center. The whole reason I started the blog was so that I could be anonymous and share my feelings. No one knows who the Marilene behind, walking and talking is and I like it that way."

Scarlett blew out a series of short breaths to regain control of herself as she experienced mental apprehension about anyone finding out who she really was.

"I don't have a problem with the program being featured, I just don't want to be featured...and especially now. I kind of enjoy living off the grid so to speak. I'm very private. My dad suggested hiring a spokesperson and I'm in full agreement with that. Would you have a problem with that?"

James reached out and lightly stroked Marilene's forearm, "I have no problems with that at all, whatever you need to make you feel comfortable. I love the idea of your program, I think it's a great fit for what I'm trying to do and I believe it has the potential to be a big hit so whatever we need to do to make it happen; I'm fine with it."

To Scarlett, James' velvety touch was comforting, yet overwhelming. Considering her circumstances, she'd been on edge for the last six months. Jaded by Carson's unforgiving manipulations, his deeds had caused her to exchange her once confident demeanor for unnecessary fears and concerns. Fear of being judged. Fear of being hurt. Fear of being found out. In a way, she needed the touch again, for a second, it washed the fears away. However, she was afraid to reach out for it.

Backing away and shielding herself from the midmorning sunshine, "We've essentially talked about everything regarding the details of your upcoming event, do you think we still need to go out to dinner?"

"I don't see why not, you've already told me you're free tonight and I've cleared my schedule for this evening, so I think dinner is still in the cards for us."

Scarlett stalled, taking time to think of an excuse. She couldn't think of any quick enough.

"Are you feeling okay, we've been walking for quite a bit and considering..."

"Considering what? Look, I'm pregnant, not handicapped. Okay."

Scarlett started walking back towards the club.

Cringing on the inside, *"Oh my goodness, what is wrong with me. I didn't mean for it to come out like that."*

"Hey, wait a minute. I know you're not handicapped; I was only making sure you weren't overdoing it."

Scarlett's mind was clearly distracted.

"I apologize; I didn't mean for it to come out like that."

Searching for a way to reverse her little war with words, she offered an attempt at reconciliation, "If the offer still stands, my choice for dinner tonight is Carol's Chophouse, it's not too far from here."

"Oh yeah, I'm very familiar with Carol's. I performed heart surgery on Carol's husband a few years ago. They treat me like a king every time I eat up there,

I'm practically family. Should I pick you up or shall I meet you there?"

"I'll meet you up there. Does seven sound okay?"

"Yes, that sounds great. Well listen, this here is my corner, I'm going to go ahead and get ready to head into work. I take it you'll be alright to make it back to the club, promise me you'll shoot me a text when you get home though."

"Okay, I will. Have a good day at work and I'll see you later at the restaurant."

James turned and sprinted towards his street. *"Oh boy, now that was interesting."*

CHAPTER 20

"*W*ell that went well. I can only imagine what James must be thinking of me after how I reacted.*"*

Taking a seat in the home office where she now ran her website; Scarlett battled with the thoughts from the morning's walk with James. *"I seriously don't have the capacity to think about this right now, I need to write my blog post for the week."*

Prior to writing the post, Scarlett noticed a couple of email notifications from the contact us email account. "Hmmm, what's this?"

Clicking through to read the email, Scarlett leaned in as she took in every word of the letter that read:

You don't know me but I feel like I've known you for a long time. Since I feel this way I hope you will receive my most sincere thanks and appreciation for what you've helped me to achieve in my life in such a short period of time.

All of my life I've struggled with my weight, I wasn't huge but I was definitely overweight. Over the years, if I'd collected a dime for every time I'd heard, "Such a pretty face...for a big girl," I'd be rich by now. Despite not feeling good about my body, I still put on a good show for everyone around me.

One year ago, my husband and I welcomed our first child and it was one of the best moments in my life. However, the additional pregnancy weight I'd gained was unwelcomed and proved to be one of the worst things in my life. I battled with gestational diabetes and high blood pressure. I felt ugly, I didn't feel like I was attractive enough for my husband anymore and I went into somewhat of a downward spiral. As a result, I started taking comfort in eating and I packed on more and more weight.

Six months ago, I was having lunch with my family in a new restaurant and I needed to use the restroom. When I arrived to the bathroom there was a line to use this petite, yet beautifully decorated restroom. The structure of the room was quite narrow as women eased by each other as they tried to exit the tiny quarters.

As I watched some women struggle to get inside one of the two stalls, I stood with one of my arms holding the other at the elbow and shifted in my spot in line. I was feeling anxious, thoughts were swirling in my head; I wondered if my body was going to fit in the doorway.

My worst fear happened. I didn't fit, I had to turn sideways to walk in and out of the door. I was mortified. Any adjective you can think of, I was. For a brief minute as the toilets flushed I broke down but I pulled it back together. My family was waiting on me at the table. I would never be able to share what I'd just experienced.

I went home that night and began to surf the web, I realized I needed to do something. Something had to change in my life. I identified those feelings I had in that bathroom as ones I never ever wanted to feel in my life again.
One search led to another search and another search and lo and behold, I came across your blog.

I don't know what you were or still are going through but I started following you because you were saying things I identified with. Through your writings, you were saying some of the very things I didn't feel I could say. When you're trying to make sense of life sometimes you don't even know how to articulate what you're feeling. In a way, you feel like a virtual big sister, someone who understands, someone looking out for me. Because of that, I started walking and talking like you did.

I started out walking alone, taking inventory of certain things in my life, core beliefs that were good and some that were not so good. I challenged myself to uphold the good ones, release the bad ones, and adopt a new set. The more I walked, the better I began to feel. My new outlook became noticeable to my family and friends and they wanted to know what I was doing and some of them started walking with me.

Over the last five months, six of us have been consistently walking and talking and we have collectively lost a combined 125 pounds. I have personally lost 25 pounds and a couple of inches.

I still have more work to do but I can tell you that today, I feel great, I'm healthy and happy. My daughter has a mother who doesn't tire easily anymore. I've been able to have more fun and add a lot more sugar and spice to my marriage.

Most importantly, I've started a journey towards learning more about God. I stopped taking comfort in food and I now take comfort in the Word of God. My walk is a daily one but through you, I've learned that I never have to walk it alone.

*I apologize for this being so long but I needed
to let you know how much I appreciate you
and how you've helped to save my life.*
~Forever Grateful

Scarlett was an emotional wreck, overwhelmed by the words of this writer. Yielding to her feelings caused Minta to stop inside the office as she walked by to see what was going on.

"Oh Lord, what has happened now? What's wrong with you? Are you in pain? Is something wrong with the baby?"

Dapping her eyes with tissue, "Calm down mama. Everything is fine. Read this."

Minta read the letter and she raised her hands towards heaven and said, "What a blessing this is. Thank you Jesus. She looks amazing, she sent you pictures and all. This is great."

Minta looked at the screen a little closer, "Hey, is this another one here?"

"I sat down to write and I saw that one, I haven't looked at anything else."

"Look Scarlett, there's another one here. Does my dear Scarlett have fan mail?"

The mother and daughter duo checked the other email and to their delight, it was another inspirational testimony and message of thanks.

"Scarlett honey, all I can say is, this is the Lord's doing and it is marvelous in our eyes."

CHAPTER 21

"Can I get you something to drink while you wait sir?"

"Yes, I'd like a glass of sweet tea."

Carmichael's was lively as the lunch crowed poured into the downtown delicatessen. George, seated and waiting perused the menu as he waited on his lunch guest.

"Hey, sorry I'm a little behind, the parking is crazy out there. You look good, how's it going?"

"Hey there Travis, things are going well. It's good to see you. I see you're wearing one of the shirts we brought last month. How's that new ride treating you?"

"Man, are you kidding me? I still can't believe you bought me a car."

"Happy to do it, I was really happy to do that for you. So, have you eaten here before?"

"No, I haven't. In all of my years living here, I've never been here to eat. In all honesty, I haven't been to a lot of the places we've been going to."

"Well, they have several good looking specials today. I'm trying to decide which one I'm going to get. I'm torn between the hot pastrami and the brisket pizza. What are you looking at getting?"

"Great minds think alike; I was looking at those same two. Maybe, I'll get one and you get the other. You cool with that?"

"Thank you for helping me out with that Travis. I thought I was going to have to risk looking greedy in front of all these people when I ordered both to eat."

Travis changed the subject and said, "I hadn't spoken to you in a few days, so I was glad when you called to have lunch."

"Yeah, sorry about not calling. Things have just been a little busy this week."

"Dude, you're retired. How busy can you be?"

"You'd be surprised. I think now I find myself busier than when I actually got up and went to work."

George prepared himself for lunch as he placed his napkin in his lap and enjoyed another glass of iced tea.

"I've been trying to be there for Scarlett, you know what I mean. We all went to her doctor's appointment the other day and found out she's having a boy."

The spark in Travis' face went dark, "Who is we all went, I didn't go. I thought you said you were going to be here for me. What happened to that?"

George's eyes tighten, his voice was strained; "I moved here didn't I."

Travis' fists were tight, his fingernails bit into his palms. "Yeah, but I keep asking you when are you going to tell your family. I don't want to keep going on like this, it's not fair to me. Are you ashamed of me?"

"No, but my family isn't ready for this. I need to do this in my time. You hear me...my time. My daughter is going through a rough patch and I'm not going to add anything else on her, Cole is in his last semester of college, and Minta has several business trips lined up."

Restaurant patrons started to stare at the rift between George and Travis.

"Sounds like a bunch of excuses to me. I can deal with you a lot better if you're honest with me and yourself for that matter. The longer this drags out, the longer it will take for you and I to become our true selves. I need that acknowledgement from you."

"Travis, I'm trying here. This is all very new to me and I'm doing the best I can. I promise when the time is right, I'll tell them but I can tell you this, the timing is not now."

The server came over and delivered a hot pastrami sandwich in front of George and the brisket pizza in front of Travis. "Here you go guys, can I get you anything else? Enjoy."

Travis dropped his napkin and stood up from the table without looking at his food.

"I'll make this easy for you man. I'm out. How 'bout this, now you don't have to choose."

Travis abruptly walked out of the restaurant causing his glass of iced tea to shatter on the floor and spray the lady seated next to George's table.

"Travis, you come back here. Travis...."

George was left alone at the table trying to clean up the mess and apologizing profusely, offering to pay for their lunch.

While the mess at the table was being cleaned up, the mess between Travis and George was only beginning.

CHAPTER 22

"Look who's here, my favorite doctor, Dr. Hartgrove. I haven't seen you in a while but it's good to see you. You would decide to come on one of our busiest nights. I don't know where I'm going to seat you. You are by yourself right?"

Carol's Chophouse was filled with wall to wall patrons looking forward to a great night at the restaurant with fine food, remarkable spirits, and sensational live entertainment.

"I'm not dining alone tonight; I'm waiting on a young lady that'll be joining me for dinner this evening."

Carol pulled James away from the other hungry and waiting customers for a more personal conversation.

"A young lady huh, are you letting me know you're dating again? I've been trying to set you up with my niece for the longest now and you keep telling me you're not ready. Does my niece now have a shot?"

James blushed a bit, "It's nothing like that, I'm not on a date, this is a friendly business dinner. Besides, you're practically like family to me, I could never go out with your niece."

Carol confronted James right on, pointing her finger in his face. "Uh-huh, not a date. You sure look very handsome tonight for this not to be a date. Like maybe you're trying to impress this woman or something and you smell nice too."

James tugged at his collar, Ms. Carol was bringing the heat down on him. All he could do was laugh at the spunky restaurateur. Saved from more of her friendly snooping, Scarlett walked up behind James and tapped him on the hand to alert him to her presence.

The dazzling blue and cayenne dress with sand colored accents adorned Scarlett's meaningful body in a way that caused heads to turn and appreciate the beauty of a woman with child.

"Oh my James, your dinner companion for this evening is stunning. Please introduce us."

James turned to make the introductions and found himself speechless for a brief second, taken by Scarlett's radiance. *"Am I looking at a cliché here or is it this ambient lighting in the restaurant, she is gorgeous, she really looks like she's glowing."*

"Marilene, this is the infamous Carol of Carol's Chophouse and Ms. Carol, this is my friend, Marilene. Ms. Carol, it was Marilene's idea to come here tonight."

"Marilene, it is a pleasure to meet you and I'm so glad you all came out tonight. It looks like I'm going to have to kick someone out of a table to get y'all a seat. We are completely booked for tonight. The band we have tonight is a crowd favorite, it's always packed whenever they perform. Let me see what I can do to get you two seated. I'll be right back."

Scarlett was still on a high from receiving the encouraging words from the two testimonials and in a way felt like celebrating. For the first time in a while, she felt free to experience life again to its fullest. Other than her family, people were now depending on her and it felt good.

"So how was the rest of your day James?"

"My day was crazy with seeing patients all day but it was good. How about yours?"

Scarlett swelled with pride, thinking back on her day. Just as she was about to explain, Carol motioned for the two of them to come over to her.

"There are no other seats available right now and we are on a two-hour wait. However, we are in the process of launching something new and I think you two maybe the first to test it out for us."

Carol escorted the couple to a cozy booth inside of the sprawling kitchen.

"This is going to be a new feature we offer; it's called the Chef's Table. Here you'll be able to have an intimate dining experience with one on one conversations with our chefs and where they will appease your palates with signature chef's creations, things not presently on the menu. We weren't going to start offering this for another week or so but since I was told this was a business dinner and the restaurant is so full, I figured I'd make an exception for you tonight. What do you think? You'll still be able to hear the band but this way, you guys can discuss your business without having to yell at each other across the table. This is a behind the scenes experience filled with surprises."

"The always amazing Ms. Carol, this is very nice of you."

"Make yourselves comfortable and Chef Roman will be out to speak with you shortly."

"Wow James, this is amazing. I guess you were right; she does treat you like royalty up here. I may need to hang out with you more often."

James' body posture was opened towards Scarlett, he nodded in agreement to her playful suggestion.

"Did I tell you there are other places that treat me like this too? You could be hanging out with me for a while."

Scarlett tilted her head giving off a slight smile. Somehow the idea of hanging out with James more often intrigued her.

"Marilene, I didn't get a chance to tell you this when you came in but I want to let you know that you look amazing."

"You clean up well yourself doc."

The playful banter between the two was interrupted by the self-introduction of Chef Roman. He challenged them to be open to the idea of exploration with their desire for food. To enjoy the culinary exploits he would create for them. Through his words and expressions, he had them hooked, they were ready to indulge in his exclusive cuisine.

"Normally, I would start you off with a bottle of wine from our signature collection, however, being mindful of my guests tonight, I recently had an opportunity to create a mocktail menu for an exclusive baby shower and I'd like to offer you something from that menu."

Chef Roman walked away and returned quickly with the mocktail menu card.

James and Scarlett scanned the menu and made their selections.

"For you my lady?"

"Chef Roman, I'd like to try the Cinderella."

"Nice choice princess and for you sir?"

"Chef Roman, I was thinking of going with the wine but hey, I think I'm going to try the coconut lime momtini."

"Excellent choices, the drinks will be up shortly. Enjoy."

After Chef Roman left, Scarlett jumped right back into their previous conversation.

"You asked me about my day earlier and I didn't get a chance to tell you but I have something to show you."

Scarlett pulled from her sand colored clutch the emails from earlier and placed them in front of James, grinning from ear-to-ear.

"Marilene, this is awesome. I hope you see how important your program is and this is exactly why I have to have it as part of the health expo we are planning. I spoke with the organizers today after we walked and they would like to set up a meeting with everyone next week. Is there a particular day that'll work for you?"

"As of right now, I don't have anything on my calendar for next week. I'm open so any day will work for me. You guys just let me know. That reminds me though, I need to start looking for the face of all of this."

Chef Roman's first course was living up to everything he'd promised. James could barely concentrate on the subject at hand for enjoying the Portobello mushroom ravioli drizzled with a chardonnay butter sauce.

"I'm so sorry, this is so good. I didn't eat today so I'm starving like Marvin right about now. Do you have a certain person or look in mind?"

"I did eat and I'm still hungry, this is beyond delicious. No, I don't have a look, all I know is that I'm not interested in being the look."

"I understand. I may have a solution for you. I have an intern working in my office and she's very passionate about wellness and heart health, not to mention, she's easy on the eyes. She does some modeling on the side to help put herself through college and I think she might be a good fit. Since she's coming from my office and I want this program to work, I'll pay her for her services."

"Oh no, I could never ask you to do that."

"Who said you asked? You aren't asking me to do anything, I'm offering you a solution so you can stay behind the scenes like you want to. All I'm trying to do is remove any hindrances that would keep this thing from happening. Let me do this."

Releasing a heavy sigh, "Can I take some time to think about it?"

"Yeah, by the time Roman brings out the next course, I'll need an answer. Is that time enough for you?"

Scarlett's playful push to James' shoulder made him drop the last bite of his ravioli onto the floor.

"Oh boy, now I'm going to have to make you pay for that. Do you know how good that ravioli was? I need an answer now."

Pressing her lips together tightly, trying to avoid answering, she answered slowly, "Alright, alright I guess you can go ahead and set that up."

"Oh well just so you know, she's already on board. I'd already set it up, I just needed you to say yes."

"You sly little fox. All jokes aside, thank you."

Chef Roman wooed them all night long with his magnificent creations, the chocolate goat cheese torte was divine and a flawless ending to an exquisite dinner.

Chef Roman came out once again to bring them each a parting gift, his dishes from the evening were now packaged for them to take home.

James and Scarlett raved about their experience to Chef Roman and heaped praise after praise on him. They thoroughly enjoyed themselves but they weren't the only ones. The baby did too.

"Omigod."

Scarlett jumped a little in her seat.

"What? Marilene, are you alright?"

Without thinking Scarlett grabbed James' hand and placed it on her stomach. Pulling him closer to her. The small space they shared had gotten smaller. No more distance between the two.

"Did you feel that; he's kicking?"

Scarlett was feeling her baby move for the first time and she was thrilled. At her last appointment, she'd asked her doctor why it hadn't happened yet. The doctor explained babies move all the time, she just wasn't aware of the sensation yet. Indicating there was no need to worry because she should start feeling the movement at any time.

That time was now and the moment was shared with James.

The adrenaline flowing through her body connected with his racing heartbeat, as his hand rested upon her stomach, she could feel his warm touch, heat emanating from his palm.

"A boy huh? Feels like you have a future soccer player in there."

Scarlett's cheeks swelled with warmth and color, she glowed with hints of rosiness and it wasn't from her MAC makeup collection.

"He wants Chef Roman to know how much he enjoyed his food."

"Marilene, I have really enjoyed this evening with you. I'm not ready to go home yet, are you? How do you feel about going for a walk downtown?"

"That sounds like a wonderful idea but I think I should probably call it a night. I really want to get home and tell my parents about the baby moving."

"Yeah, that was pretty special, I can understand that. Rain check?"

"You bet. Let's talk soon. Thanks for a wonderful evening, doctor."

CHAPTER 23

"I'm home. Mama, daddy...where are you guys? I have some news."

Scarlett searched through the house to find her parents enjoying their evening poolside.

"Hello, hello out here. Is this where the party is tonight?"

"C'mon, sit down and join us. So, how was your date, I mean dinner?"

Scarlett shook her head at her father, "How many times do I need to tell you guys I didn't go on a date?"

George laughed with concession, "I amended my statement, didn't I?"

"Indeed you did daddy." Scarlett stood up and kissed her father on his head and then poured a glass of iced tea.

Minta chimed in, "You still haven't answered though, you know we want to know what happened so how was your dinner girl?"

Scarlett had an intense desire to share the news with her parents but she was purposefully trying to down play her excitement for them because she knew they were interested.

Stalling for one more minute, biting down on a smile and looking out into the calm waters of the pool, Scarlett shouted out, "Dinner was, A-MAZ-ING."

Saying those words out loud, admitting she'd had a good time was liberating. Scarlett felt a sudden need to run, jump, scream and simply whoop it up. Her behavior was infectious, her parents stood up and started dancing, even though they didn't know why they were dancing.

"I felt the baby kick for the first time tonight at dinner."

Minta stopped in the middle of her dance and George belted out a holler and jumped into the pool.

"George, you are crazy. Why did you jump in the pool with all of your clothes on?"

"I don't know, I got caught up in all of the hype and I didn't know what else to do. The baby kicked tonight. I'm so happy, I literally didn't know what to do with myself."

Both Minta and Scarlett laughed and said, "Apparently."

George swam one quick lap, in his clothes and then hopped out. Minta was there waiting for him with a towel.

Drying off, George came to a realization. "So Scarlett, if you felt the baby kick tonight at dinner that means you experienced that moment with Dr. Hartgrove, was he there?"

Scarlett tried to hide her expression with her hair but it didn't work.

"Yes, he was there and I have to say, he was awesome throughout the entire dinner and feeling my stomach."

Minta clutched her chest, "He felt your stomach; he felt the kick? I want to feel it too."

"Just like daddy, when it happened, I didn't know how to react and the first thing I did was grabbed his hand so he could feel it....it was nice. Glad there weren't any pools around or I might have jumped in like crazy over here."

Minta inched closer to Scarlett and knelt down beside her, aligning herself in front of Scarlett's stomach. "Hey in there, hey little boy, it's your Mimi, we are so looking forward to meet you. I can't wait to get my hands on you and spoil you rotten."

Minta's words must have resonated with the bundle of joy because he responded in-kind with a kick.

"Oh my goodness, he kicked. He likes what his Grammy has to say already."

The mommy-to-be and her parents were overjoyed at the baby's first kicks, it seemed to crystalize the notion that a living, breathing baby was actually inside and would be making his way to the outside in a few short months.

CHAPTER 24

"*It's been a week and I haven't heard from Travis. He hasn't called and he hasn't returned any of my phone calls. I guess he wants me to come chasing after him.*"

George was up and out of the house early before any of the ladies of the house were up and moving around.

On the drive over to Travis' apartment, he tried calling again. Still no answer from Travis.

"*I guess he is really mad at me. I just need him to give me a little more time before I spring this on my family. Why can't he understand that? Out of everything I've done for him since I've been here, why can't he just give me that?*"

George moved Travis to a new apartment not long after arriving in Jordan. His apartment was connected to a private garage so George was unable to see if Travis was home based on his car being in the parking lot.

Parking his car away from Travis' apartment, George walked around throughout the complex to the newly acquired accommodations. He didn't want to chance being seen by anyone and especially tipping Travis off to his presence.

One knock, no answer.

Two knocks at the door. Still no answer.

The secret knock they shared, still no answer at the door.

"Travis, if you're in there, open up. It's me. You've proved your point. I'm here so open up the door."

From what George could tell, there was no movement inside the bachelor pad.

"Should I leave him a note?"

Dialing Travis once more to see if he could hear his phone ring inside.

George heard nothing.

"He asked me if I wanted a key but I never got one because I never thought we'd be having these type of issues. Now I know I should've gotten a key. He's not here so I guess I'll leave."

Upset for not being able to connect with Travis, George took out his frustrations on the road. He sped out of the complex and turned the corner recklessly not even noticing Travis' car turning in.

Travis, however, did notice George tearing out of the parking lot.

"What's he doing here? I guess he doesn't understand that I'm not talking to him unless he's ready to tell his family about our relationship."

CHAPTER 25

"I hope y'all youngins' ate your Wheaties this morning because my honey and I are in full swing today and we are ready to ace y'all out and put a grand slam on y'alls behinds."

Carson was talking full loads of trash to his younger brother, Christian and his fiancé, Courtney.

"You can stop it with all of the tennis jargon, just come on out here and get your butt beat like a respectable man. Stop it with all that jaw-jacking. That's all you've ever been, all talk."

Courtney was sensing Christian was getting agitated by Carson and she came over to lighten the mood between the two brothers.

"Who wants to make a little wager on this showdown at the court today?"

"Courtney dear, how dare you bring up betting out here? Someone might hear you, we are men and women of the cloth...we don't make wagers. You of all people should know that."

Courtney Davis was the youngest daughter of the Davis family in Jordan, Mississippi, who had a thriving ministry in the South. Courtney and Christian met in college. He proposed at their graduation. Courtney decided to follow him to California so they could get married. Their wedding date was fastly approaching.

Until the wedding, the arrangement was Courtney was to live with the senior Montgomery's while Christian lived on the other side of town.

Another ministerial dynasty was being properly aligned.

"Geesh, I was only trying to add an element of fun to the game. You two are really something else. Besides, who is going to hear us out here? Give me a break, let's just play the game."

Carson announced before the first serve with great command, "We're playing the best three out of five, may the best couple win."

After five long arduous sets, the younger couple, Christian and Courtney proved to be victorious on the courts, beating out their competition. The sibling-couple rivalry was now in full effect.

Throwing down his racket, "Rematch...I demand a rematch."

"Now you ladies see what I mean, Carson can never take his beat downs like a man. He can dish it but he so can't take it."

Carson narrowed his eyes and looked down his nose at his younger brother, "*I don't know who he thinks he is talking to me like that in front of my wife.*"

Christian continued with his jabs at his brother, rubbing the loss of the match more in Carson's face. "We beat y'all on the court, maybe Courtney and I should give you two a run for the pulpit and see who wins that match up as well."

"Clearly, you have no idea who you are dealing with Christian, you better take your win here on the courts and run along and get married and leave the church business to me. Trust me on that, I got this…all of it."

Carson became hostile as Christian questioned his ability to lead Wondrous Works. Carson was feeling somewhat threatened, he'd done too much to assume the highest position at the church and nothing or no one was going to get in his way.

Rebekkah intervened between the two, "Okay, okay guys that's enough, let's go inside and grab some lunch."

"And the gangs all here, who won…the newlyweds or the engaged couple?"

Christian and Courtney took a victory dance around the kitchen before they answered the patriarch of the Montgomery clan, "We did, whoop, whoop."

Regina joined the group in the kitchen as they prepared themselves for lunch.

"What's all the racket for? Pardon my pun. Who won the game?"

Christian and Courtney repeated their dance and chant for Regina while Carson and Rebekkah sat and watched.

Regina laughed, "My sons are so competitive; they always have been. Going all the way back from when they were little boys."

"I'm not competitive mama, Carson is just a sore loser." Christian made sure to place special emphasis on the word, loser as Courtney stood behind him and made an "L" shape on her forehead.

Carson slammed his water bottle down on the table, "Oh, I got your loser, you better back off Christian. I'm about tired of you."

"Um Carson, look you and Rebekkah invited us to play with y'all not the other way around. Just take your loss like a man and be done with it. You've always bragged about your back hand, how tennis was your game. Well guess what, you just got beat at your own game. I think that might be a sign if you ask me."

Carson sneered, "Good thing no one is asking you."

Bishop Montgomery put a stop to all of the bickering, "Enough. Clarice has prepared a nice lunch for us. We are going to eat it and we are going to fellowship and be nice towards one another. If you guys playing tennis is going to turn my courts into a battle ground, don't come back and play. You all are much too old for fighting on the playground. The two of you are acting like little children instead of men. Now let us pray."

For a few moments, the table sat in complete silence. The sound of forks hitting the plates was the only sound to be heard.

Regina took it upon herself to get the table talking again. "So Courtney and Christian, how's the wedding planning going...or should I just be asking Courtney?"

"Mama Montgomery, things are going very well, couldn't be better. Christian and I will be flying home next week for our tastings, the food, the cake, the drinks, you name it. It helps having a wedding planner at our church, she is handling everything and I couldn't be happier. I tell her what I want and she makes it happen. With my daddy's check book of course. With five months left before the wedding, I want to make sure everything is perfect, next week's visit is a simple face to face touch point. I'm very excited because I'll get to have what I hope is the final fitting for my dress, hopefully, I'll be able to pick it up then."

"Next week, wait a minute. You will be back in time for the luncheon though, right Courtney?"

"Yes ma'am, but of course. We'll definitely be back in time. Mama Montgomery, I wouldn't miss it, in fact I'm actually looking forward to it. I know how much you've been working on it."

Across the table, Rebekkah scoffed and under her breath, slipped out, "Suck up," as if she was coughing.

Keeping a careful watch on Rebekkah, Regina saw what she did, "Did you say something Rebekkah?"

"No ma'am, I think some of my food went down the wrong pipe."

"Uh-huh, I'm sure it did young lady. Well, there it is folks, both ladies will be at the luncheon. It's going to be a wonderful event."

Carson winked at Rebekkah, the Bishop smiled at Regina, and Christian smiled over at Courtney and rubbed her hand.

Everything was all settled or so it appeared.

The familial scene was picturesque around the table, however, it was hard to ignore the empty seat at the elongated dinner table.

The empty seat belonged to the one and only, baby of the family, Cayden-James Montgomery.

CHAPTER 26

"**W**ake up. State your name and number."

"Cayden-James Montgomery, number 309729."

"Alright young man, you're done for now. We shall do this all again in two hours."

Having already served eighteen months in his federal prison camp, a prison for the privileged, Cayden-James still found it hard to adjust to the mandatory night checks.

Grateful to his post-conviction specialist for lobbying for his accommodations, Montgomery, Alabama seemed to be fitting for a Montgomery man; yet he was willing to pay anything to not be there in the first place. Alabama was a long way away from the old wine country.

For the inmates, every night the lights went out at ten o'clock sharp, however, the guards were required to verify each inmate's physical presence at certain intervals throughout the night. The nightly checks starting at midnight, then at three, and again at five in the morning were still quite hard on Cayden-James.

Plopping back down on his bed, Cayden-James blew out his frustrations in puffs of air through his mouth.

The dark circles under his eyes matched the dry and grittiness they had from lack of sleep.

Often times he would drift back off to sleep by obsessing over his crimes that landed him in what he affectionately called, the bin for sin.

"How on earth did I end up here?"

While it was hard for him to fathom being locked up and away from all of the abundant extravagance for which he was accustomed, he knew exactly how he ended up in the minimum-security prison facility.

With his whole life ahead of him, Cayden-James was looking to chart his own course. Overshadowed by two older brothers who seemed to have it all together, he set up unrealistic expectations of himself in an effort to make his parents proud.

He had no desire to accept the mantle passed down through generations of Montgomery men to pastor. He did have every desire to make an imprint on society and leave something behind that would be known as his.

Unfortunately, ministry was a source of strife for him. He chose to see the negative aspects of the church, not the good. Cayden-James loved God but had deep seeded issues with the church. He felt like religion was used as a form of control and not the freedom having a relationship with Christ brings. The stained glass windows everyone admired branded a stain on his soul. His attempt to reconcile the dysfunction of the church against his destiny in Christ set him off in a whirlwind of confusion.

"I had it all and I threw it all away...and for what? To end up here in this hell hole. Man, I was a senior in

college, set to graduate in about a year and I blew it. If I could take it all way, I would."

As a young computer whiz, Cayden-James turned an idea he had into a multi-million dollar business that he ran out of his off-campus apartment.

The thoughts from the past ransacked his mind, tonight he's not only a prisoner in the system but also a prisoner to his own mind.

All it took was reading an article about Bitcoins in the school's library and he was hooked. He saw an opportunity and he took it.

Uncovering a missing element within the Bitcoin world would make him a mastermind and he went for it. Discovering the vulnerabilities within the trading platforms he was on to something and something big. Creating the world's first back up service for Bitcoin purchasers and their digital wallets was brilliant.

The business would become a cloud-based Bitcoin backup service where the system offers various layers of protection such as military-grade firewalls, high availability and encrypted storage, along with off-sight and offline backup solutions.

"Oh my goodness. I got caught up trying to be better than my brothers and I got greedy. My desire to show them up started to consume me. Why wasn't I happy with just doing something neither one of them could ever do or come up with? I needed so badly to do something greater than Carson and Christian and make mama and the Bishop proud that I sacrificed the values I once held near and dear to me."

Scores of people joined his service, the money Cayden-James made was like rain falling from the sky during a hurricane storm. Articles were now being written about him, no one really knew who he was though. He became known as the new prince of Bitcoins.

"The first time I realized I had access to all of the digital wallets of my customers, I smiled and thanked God for allowing me to have such a successful business. I had done it. I wish I would have left it there."

More and more people signed up for the service. Things couldn't have been going better. The analytics proved he filled a need within the Bitcoin niche and marketplace. People needed what he had to offer and they were signing up in droves.

"Boy, I tell you...there's a reason the bible tells you to take your thoughts captive because the more I looked at all of those wallets and their balances, I started thinking, who's going to notice a little skimmed off here or there.[6] Waking up every morning and seeing what I'd accomplished the night before became like a drug to me, I could really care less about the money; I was enticed by seeing what I was able to do by myself."

More times than not, he mentally berated himself over his poor decisions, constantly thinking of ways to make things right, *"I don't know how, but someday, I'm going to turn this into something positive. I may never get to mail them but I think I've written just about everyone that I stole from and apologized."*

Most people don't start out with the wrong intentions. However, one bad deed breeds another, sin

---

[6] **2 Corinthians 10:5**: *"Casting down imaginations, and every high thing that exalteth itself against the knowledge of God, and bringing into captivity every thought to the obedience of Christ"*

begets sin and before you know it, you're caught up in a really bad situation.

Skimming the money took on a life of its own and Cayden-James started investing the digital currency in overnight exchanges and making gigantic returns on the funds. Until...

"Who knew that Middle Eastern crisis was going to happen? Man, that is a day I shall never forget. I had been investing the skimmed off funds from my sweep accounts and I was heavily leveraged in all sorts of positions but mainly in oil futures. The crisis caused all of my investments to drop dramatically and I lost everybody's money...money that wasn't mine. Lord knows we needed peace in the Middle East that day."

The familiar dullness in his chest and the heaviness filling his body arrived like clockwork. The weight of his transgressions plagued him daily, he needed a way out...but how?

"I knew I was in trouble, I had lost so much money. The anonymity from the Bitcoin business made me think I could shut everything down and go about my life like nothing happened. It only took the Feds two weeks before they showed up knocking at my door and it was a wrap. The hardest thing I had to do was call my parents. Now, I'm left here wondering, why did this have to happen to me?"

"It's your five o'clock wake up call. Get up. State your name and number."

In obedience to the command, standing from a night of tormenting thoughts in a fog of hazy disgrace, the tiniest cub of the Montgomery tribe softly replied, "Cayden-James Montgomery, number 309729, sir."

CHAPTER 27

Stretching out through his long wingspan from a restful night of sleep, *"It's such a beautiful day outside, I think I may actually go for a walk this morning before I go into work. I need to do a little walking and talking today. But who am I going to talk to?"*

"Good morning Ms. Anita, I'm calling to check on you and see how you are doing while I'm out on my morning walk."

"Oh, good morning son, I'm doing fine. Thanks again for the dinner the other night, I really enjoyed myself and you did a wonderful job honoring Cheryl on such short notice."

Pounding the pavement and talking to Ms. Anita was refreshing, it was just what the doctor ordered.

"Have you given any more thought to what I told you the other night James?"

"What? We talked about a lot of things Ms. Anita."

"Boy, you know what I'm talking about, don't play around with me."

Pretending to laugh it off, James answered, "I have thought about what you said."

"It's time for you to move on son, Cheryl would want you to be happy and I want that for you too. You deserve all the happiness life has to offer."

"Ms. Anita, I am happy."

"You know what I mean James. You were about to propose to Cheryl so you were apparently ready to get married and by now I'm sure you two would've been working on giving me a grandchild. All I'm saying is that I'd like to see you move on with that part of your life."

Heat rose up through his ears, his chest caved, and he confessed his heart.

"I think I've met someone who has caught my eye, I definitely feel a vibe or some sort of connection with her but -."

"But what James, what reason are you going to come up with son?"

"She's pregnant."

Unmoved by the revelation, Anita didn't skip a beat.

"Do you know the circumstances around her pregnancy?"

"No ma'am, unfortunately I don't. It's been hard to approach her about it. I know there is some drama somewhere because she's eluded to it but I don't know the details."

In a loving tone, Anita inquired, "Well James, let me ask you this, have you prayed about it at all?"

"No, I haven't. I don't think I was going to bother the big guy about this because she's pregnant which means there is a baby daddy not too far removed from her and I wasn't sure if I wanted to be a part of that."

"Yet, you're talking to me about her."

James stopped from his walk to catch his breath because he needed it from laughing so hard at his spiritual mother.

"Touché', touché' Ms. Anita...you got me."

"Sounds like to me you need to pray and talk to the Lord about this situation and then if you feel the need to know more, find a way to ask her about what's going on."

"As always, you're right."

"James, I'm curious about something you said. Let's just say things go well with you and this woman, do you think you'd have a problem raising another man's baby? Is that what concerns you?"

Struggling to find the right words, James pressed his lips together in a slight grimace, "I would be lying if I didn't say I haven't thought about it and what that might mean for me. On the flip side, I've never told you this but my father is not my biological father. Derrick Hartgrove met my mother when I was seven months old and they married shortly before my first birthday. On my first birthday, everything was finalized, Derrick adopted me and changed my last name to Hartgrove."

"I never knew that James, I just assumed...."

"No one really knows, I found out on my eighteenth birthday but it didn't matter to me, as far as I was concerned, he is my father. My brothers and sisters don't even know."

"That is incredible James. Do you know anything about your biological father?"

"Nope, never asked. For whatever reason, Derrick found my mother alone with a seven-month old son, she was in her last semester in college and she would take me to classes with her. If the man who played his part in getting me here could leave her like that for another man to find her and never once tried to contact her, there isn't anything I want to know about him. I thank God every day for Derrick Hartgrove, the real man he put in my life."

"Boy, oh boy, you have blown me away here today. Your father is a good man and he's your dad in every sense of the word. James, I need to go but do what I said and I'm going to do what I know how to do and that is pray. I'm praying for you son, keep me posted, and I'll talk with you soon."

Circling the roads ready to head back home, James began another conversation.

"Lord have mercy, I just shared my family secret with Ms. Anita and she thinks I need to talk to you. Lord, is there something to my attraction towards Marilene? Is there a greater purpose for why she has now entered into my life? Lord, I'm going to trust in You with all of my heart and I'm going to lean not to my own understanding in this situation but I need to acknowledge you in all of my ways as it relates to Marilene so that you might direct my path. In Jesus' name. Amen."

Stopping briefly to savor the moment of his conversation with the "man upstairs" James heard, "James, James, is that you?"

Turning to hear who might be calling his name, he did a double take, the caller was the lovely Marilene.

Looking up to the sky he muttered under his breath, "Hey big guy, you sure work fast."

"I see you're out walking and talking this morning. I must be rubbing off on you. I'm out here trying to get my walk in for the day."

"In more ways than I think you realize."

"Oh yeah, well I told you I love the concept and if I'm going to promote it at the health expo then I don't need to just talk the talk without walking the walk. Oh yes, there is no need to pardon my pun, I meant every word."

Scarlett issued a swat towards James, "You're funny, I actually happen to like your puns."

James glistened in the sunlight as the springtime sun reflected in the beads of sweat that dripped from his body, not willing to admit it aloud but Scarlett liked that too.

"Really now, is that right? Try this one on then. Do you know the reason I became a doctor? Well, a long time ago, I used to be a banker but I lost interest."

"Okay, now that was just dumb...you are hilarious."

James was enjoying seeing Marilene smile, he found himself wanting to see more of it. Although, he needed to know more.

"Speaking of the expo, are we still on schedule to have the meeting with your staff tomorrow morning?"

"Yes ma'am, we are if you are."

"That sounds great, I think I'm actually getting excited about it."

"That's awesome. I'm looking forward to seeing all that may come out of this Ms. Marilene. Hey look, I need to get going but it has been a pleasure walking into you today, literally, and I look forward to seeing you tomorrow. I may call you later, if that's alright with you?"

Smiling and waving goodbye, she responded, "I'd like that."

CHAPTER 28

"**H**ey honey, I was thinking."

Peering down over his morning newspaper, "Oh Lord, Minta's been thinking."

"Oh hush George. See there, now you make me not even want to tell you."

Grabbing Minta up in a nice bear hug, George reassures her, "You know I was only joking with you honey. I'm all ears, what's on your mind sweetheart?"

"Well, since the baby will be here in a few months and I'm wrapping up my practice with these last few consultations, I was thinking that before I go out on my next consult you and I could go away for a few days. What do you think?"

George danced a little jig and kissed Minta, "I think that's the best idea I've heard today honey. You'll be okay leaving Scarlett here for a few days?"

"You know; I think she might enjoy the break away from us. I know that I've been smotherly-motherly since she arrived but she seems to have a different light in her eyes now. I like what I'm seeing, I think she'll be okay."

"I agree and in that case, when are we going and where are we going?"

"Now that I know you're fine with it, I'll call our travel agent and see if they can recommend a great last minute trip for us."

Clapping her hands together and squealing, "I'm so excited George; we need this little getaway. So much has been going on; I just want to sneak away with you for a few days."

Twirling his bride around and bracing her for the big dip, "You know what they say, happy wife; happy life. In all of our years together, I know that to be true. My life is much better when you are happy."

CHAPTER 29

"I can't believe we stayed up all night talking. Funny thing is, I don't even feel tired. I'm sure it will catch up with me later though."

Yawning through the phone, "I'm not so lucky, I feel extremely tired this morning. You wore me out last night girl, but you know what, I'd do it all over again. How long before you get here?"

"According to the GPS, I'll be at your office in about seven minutes."

"Drive carefully, I'll see you in a bit. I need to do something before you get here. When you get here, just knock, one of the girls will be waiting to let you in."

"Okay cool, see you shortly."

Scarlett emerged from her car donning a navy and white striped dress that caressed her newfound blossoming curves. Stepping up to knock at the office door wasn't necessary as Sarah, the office manager was standing at the door anticipating her arrival.

"Good morning, you must be Marilene. I'm the office manager here at Dr. Hartgrove's office, it's so nice to meet you. Dr. Hartgrove along with the rest of the crew is waiting in the conference room for you."

Scarlett walked into the conference room where the breakfast meeting was to take place to find the largest bouquet of flowers she'd ever seen in front of a chair that was clearly marked for her.

James stood to greet her and escort her to her seat, whispering in her ear, "No sleep and you still managed to look flawless."

Making sure she was comfortable in her chair, James went around the room and introduced everyone.

"Marilene Watson, this is Alicia Hamilton, the event planner for the health fair/expo, Raquel Lewis, the intern I was telling you about, I think you met Sarah already, our office manager, and last but certainly not least, Reese and Ryan Calhoun from R. Calhoun Marketing and Associates, they will be handling the marketing and public relations efforts on behalf of my office for this upcoming event."

Immediately a light bulb went off in Alicia's head, "My goodness, you have quite a familiar face to me, I feel like I've seen you somewhere before."

"Leaning away from Alicia in an attempt evade further interest in her familiar looks, Scarlett shook her head, "Um, not real sure, I'm new to the area and I haven't met a lot of people so, maybe I do just happen to have one of those faces."

Alicia moved in closer, she wouldn't let her suspicion go, "Yeah, maybe, I'm sure I'll figure it out, hopefully it'll come to me before you leave here today."

Lifting her chin to appear confident, Scarlett could not escape the prickling she felt in her scalp and the quivering in her stomach and this time it was from the baby.

"Maybe this isn't such a good idea, I can't afford for anyone to figure out who I am. I can't risk the

Montgomery's finding out my location, especially now with the baby."

Slipping out of consciousness, wrestling with her own thoughts, she was ushered back into reality by James who gave her a nod of encouragement and a smile that melted her heart. *"I'm sure I'm overreacting, I just need to chill out, I'm certain there's nothing to worry about. Everything is going to be fine."*

Scarlett found it hard to concentrate on the meeting but through it all, she made it to the end.

"We have about fifteen minutes before our office opens and I'd like to thank everyone for coming out so early for this breakfast meeting. I think we made a lot of progress here today, each year has been better than the one before so I know this one is going to be great. This is the right team to make it happen and I'm excited. I'll see you all next month for another touch point meeting."

The date for the health fair had been confirmed, Raquel was now the face for the Walking and Talking campaign and the marketing and public relations plans had been approved. It was official, Scarlett's program was going to be the featured event at the expo.

Dr. Hartgrove thanked each of his guests one by one as Scarlett grabbed her things to leave.

"Marilene, allow me to walk you out."

Scarlett turned to say goodbye to everyone and noticed everyone was still around with the exception of Alicia.

"Sure thing, will you please tell Alicia I said goodbye and I look forward to working with her."

James and Scarlett walked outside, patients were already driving up for their top of the morning appointments.

Being a gentleman and opening Scarlett's car door, "So, what are your plans for the rest of the day, pretty lady? Where do you want your flowers ma'am, front seat or the back seat?"

"Not too much, I have a little running around to do but nothing major. The flowers are beautiful by the way; you didn't have to do that you know."

"There you go, always telling me what I didn't have to do. The correct thing to say is thank you for the flowers. I'm only kidding. A little running around huh? Well, if you aren't too tired, would you like to catch dinner later?"

"If I didn't know any better, I'd think you're trying to fatten me up. I'm already big as a house, I don't need any help from you."

"No, not at all. You can't tell me after all we talked about last night you don't enjoy hanging out with me. C'mon, you know you want to hang with me."

Waving James off in a flippant way, "Whatever man. Call me later and we'll see what's up."

Laughing at her refusal to speak the truth, James replied, "I'll do just that Ms. Lady and I expect you to answer when I call."

"Okay, it's really time for me to go now, the doctor is losing his mind. Goodbye."

Walking back inside, the office staff noticed James was whistling. He walked back in with a sleek stride that drew the attention to Alicia.

"My, my...you seem mighty happy with yourself right now James. You and I have been working together on this health expo for a couple of years now and I haven't seen you this happy in a long time."

"We had a great meeting this morning, didn't we Alicia? Based on everything I heard today, this should be our best one, don't you think?"

"Yes, I do think so. I think it's going to be great. Hey, I invited you out to dinner with some friends a few weeks ago and you couldn't make it and you promised me you'd come the next time. Well, that same group of friends is getting together again tonight and I'd like to cash in my rain check. What say you Dr. Hartgrove?"

"Why did I tell her I'd go out with her and her friends? They would decide to go out tonight when I have asked Marilene out for this evening. I'd much rather go out with Marilene if she's available. How am I to get out of this?"

"Oh yeah, I remember that. Is it okay if I keep you posted towards the end of the day? I didn't get much sleep last night and I have a full day of seeing patients."

Breaking eye contact with James, Alicia's face went slack and paled slightly, "Sure, of course. I understand. Let me know later then, I'd really like it if you could come out."

The first patient of the day was in the examination room waiting on him, "Hey Alicia, I will definitely let you know later, okay. I'm going to get going but thanks again, everything's going to be great this year. I can feel it."

Reaching in for a brief hug, James patted Alicia on the back and left her there to gather her things.

Strolling towards her car, on the way out of the door, she pulled out her phone, "Yeah mom, it's me. Give me a call when you can. Talk to you later. Bye."

CHAPTER 30

"Courtney and Christian are flying out today, and I want to take my beautiful wife out to dinner. What do you think about that sweetheart?"

"That sounds like a great idea honey but I have a meeting tonight with the caterer who will be preparing for Saturday's luncheon. It's always crazy around here this time. You understand don't you, honey?"

Bishop Montgomery's voice dropped, "How about this. Why don't you have your meeting and then we can still go out once you're done."

Regina cited her plans for Saturday and listed more things she needed to do that night, "This is my one big event that I'm responsible for sweetie and you know this. I have first ladies from all over coming in for this and as the hostess, I need for everything to be perfect. I don't want anything to go wrong. My name is on the line here, your name is on the line, in fact, Wondrous Works' name is all on the line."

Shaking his head in disapproval, he couldn't keep his thoughts to himself, he had to let his feelings be known, "I understand you having your event, what I don't understand is why you can't move your meetings to another day in order to go and have a nice evening out with your husband. I mean for goodness sakes Regina, you've been having this luncheon for years, it shouldn't be that hard to do by now, am I right about it?"

"Eugene, I can't believe you right now. The luncheon is this weekend, you and I can go out anytime. Let me take care of this and get this off my plate and I promise after this is over, you and I can spend as much time together as we need to. Okay, please can you give me that?"

Refusing to be bought off through her kind words and conciliatory thoughtfulness, Eugene walked out of the room in silence.

CHAPTER 31

"Carson. Hey, are you alright?" Peeking under the covers to check on her husband, Rebekkah poked Carson until he responded.

"What's wrong with you girl, why are you bothering me? I'm trying to sleep. Leave me alone."

"I'm checking on you. It's not like you to sleep in like this so I was concerned. We have a lot to do today or have you forgotten?"

Rolling back over in bed and covering his entire body with the cozy goose-down feathers, "I'm sorry. I think that tennis match wore me out yesterday more than I want to admit. I have a headache and I'm really tired. I was only trying to catch up on a little rest."

Sitting down next to Carson, Rebekkah stroked his scalp, her fingers glided through his wavy locks. She loved playing in his hair. Carson had great hair, it was a trait of every Montgomery man.

"Well, you're usually up early in the mornings, and I mean up in more ways than one, if you catch my drift. However, when you didn't wake me for our morning trysts and slept through me getting up and dressed, I knew something was off with you."

"Are you saying you missed daddy this morning, is that what you're trying to tell me baby?"

Carson always seemed to know what to do and say to put Rebekkah at ease. She giggled like a school girl, she ate up everything Carson did and said.

"All I was trying to get you to understand is that if I see my husband sleeping in when he knows we have a lot of things to do, then shouldn't I be concerned and check on him?"

Wanting her to stop talking, Carson slid his hands up Rebekkah's legs, stopping short at the point of her no return. She became inarticulate as her breath quickened under his masterful touch.

"You don't have to worry your pretty little head, daddy is definitely now "up" and doesn't care that you are already dressed. Don't you know I can make your clothes fall off at my command?"

Pulling Rebekkah in closer, it was like he'd performed a magic trick, her clothes were now off.

Tickled pink, Rebekkah wondered aloud in amazement, "How did that happen?"

Laughing in a deep, sensual way, "I'm Carson baby. You know I got it like that. That's how I got you isn't it?"

He was about to say Scarlett but luckily, he caught himself before he ruined the mood.

"Why would I be thinking about Scarlett at a time like this? I've got to get my act together. Maybe if I could just find out she's okay then I wouldn't be tripping like this."

Not noticing his brief retreat to his thoughts, Rebekkah kissed him with seductive strokes, "I really didn't come in here for this and while I hate to admit it. That is how you got me and guess what? I want you to get me now."

Furtively looking Rebekkah's exposed body up and down and drawing attention to his lips with a smooth lick, he obliged, "Your wish is my command baby."

CHAPTER 32

"Oh wow, I can't believe he actually showed up."

Alicia excused herself from her friends to go and greet James.

"Well hello there handsome, you actually showed up. I'm so glad you decided to stop by."

Stepping in to give a warm hug, "What do you mean, you seem surprised. I don't know about anybody else but I'm a man of my word. Plus, for all that you do for me, this is the least I could do. I told you I'd try and make it. That's what friends are for, right?"

Alicia enjoyed the hug, she lingered on him a bit by straightening his collar, "Hold on a minute, let me help you with that. You can't be going around my friends looking crazy."

Alicia and James walked over to the rowdy bunch enjoying the camaraderie of their shared passions of sociable tastes for good food and good wine, "The Bon Vivants" as they called themselves.

Alicia gushed as she made the introductions, "Hey everybody, this is Dr. James Hartgrove."

Gracious in his greeting, "Please call me James."

"See what I mean guys, he's so modest. Well James, here is the gang, I'd like for you to meet my dear friends, Cassandra, Carlos, Lyla, and Jonathan."

James' sophisticated, yet down-to-earth demeanor seemed to put the crew around him at ease. He was an immediate hit with the group.

Cassandra was particularly impressed with James, she cozied up next to him, "Alicia, where have you been hiding this tall glass of deliciousness?"

"Cassandra, you're a mess. I haven't been hiding him. He's been hiding from me. I told you I tried to get him to come the last time and he didn't show up."

"Well, I'm here now aren't I?"

Cassandra moved in closer, "Indeed, you are. Are you hungry, do you need something to drink James?"

Tugging at his collar, James replied, "Nah, I'm fine for now but thanks."

Pointing towards herself, "Alrighty then, if you need anything and I mean anything, you just let me know. I'm your girl." She ended her offer with a wink.

James maneuvered his way and slid out from under Cassandra's grip, searching for the male compadres in the group.

Jonathan made room for James, "So James. Alicia has been telling us about the work you're doing with your annual expo. I hear it's coming up again. I'm a chiropractor, is there anything I can do to help you out?"

James lit up from hearing Carlos speak about his upcoming event, "Yeah man, plans for this year's expo are already underway, we had a great meeting this morning. I'm sure you guys are aware of how talented Alicia is when it comes to planning events. I don't know where I'd be without her help."

Eavesdropping in on the guy's conversation while still trying to maintain conversation with the girls, Alicia blushed upon hearing the kind compliments about her work.

"Hey man, you think you might be interested in being a vendor out at the expo, there will be a lot of foot traffic out there. Last year, we had about twenty thousand attendees and we are anticipating more this year. How about this, I'll even give you the new friend discount."

Carlos raised his glass in agreement, "That would be great. Check this out now, it takes you coming here to invite me to be a part of this project; Alicia's been working on this event for years and has never invited a brother to become a vendor."

"Well, in her defense, she wears a lot of hats but she does it gracefully. She always seems to manage to pull off an awesome event and she keeps all of the drama away from me. I'm sure it just slipped her mind."

Alicia missed hearing Carlos say, "Yeah, Alicia...she is pretty amazing."

Still trying to listen to the guys but keep up with the girls, Alicia rolled her eyes and scoffed at Carlos' seemingly cut to her but smiled at James' comments.

She was enjoying what she was hearing from James until....

"Each year I look for ways to build upon the successes we've had from the year before and man, this year I'm so excited about one of the features we will be showcasing."

Carlos and Jonathan closed in the ranks on James to hear him better, "Sounds like something big, can you tell us more about it?"

James spent the next half hour talking about the health fair. The guys were engaged and intrigued, Alicia was not. Bitterness built up with in her as she watched her friends respond favorable to someone they didn't even know.

In the midst of his explanation to his new found friends, James received a text:

"Hey u, is there still a plan 4 dinner?"

He responded back instantly.

"I'm out w/some friends, will call u soon."

Seeing the text from Scarlett took his level of excitement up another notch but he didn't even realize how animated he was.

To Alicia, he was a bit too happy.

"He's supposed to be talking about the health fair and the wonderful job I'm doing but all he's doing is going on and on about that pot-bellied pig, Marilene...or if that's even her name. Yeah, I think I need to bring him in on some things."

Excusing herself from the table with the ladies, Alicia sauntered her little self over to the guys.

"I'm sorry to interrupt this meeting at the gentleman's club but James do you mind if I speak with you for a moment?"

"Sure thing. Maybe you can walk me out? I actually need to get going."

"You're leaving already?"

"Yes Alicia. I said I'd stop by and I have. I now need to move on to the next thing."

James walked around and said his good-byes and exchanged contact information with the guys.

Cassandra made sure to leave her business card with James as well. "Good-bye handsome, it has been a real pleasure meeting you. You should call me sometime."

Alicia pulled James away from the group and they walked outside.

"What's up, what do you need to talk to me about?"

Kicking at the tires of James' car, she looked up at him, "After today's meeting and having the chance to actually meet Marilene, I was wondering how much do you know about her? I mean, you seem to be putting A LOT of stock in her and promoting her for your event. I've been trying to figure out why she needs a spokesperson, seriously, give me a break...who is she?"

The cross-examination caught James by surprise, "Hey young lady, hold up a bit. All I can tell you is that what I know about her is cool, she comes from good people and most importantly for right now, her campaign is going to be a nice touch to this year's expo. Not to mention, I happen to think she's an amazing person."

"Why do I feel like I'm defending Marilene to Alicia, why is she even talking to me about her?"

"I just wondered where you found her from because something about her doesn't add up to me."

James' head flinched back slightly, "Am I missing something here Alicia?"

Not taking too kindly to his tone, Alicia flashed a stack of folded up papers onto the hood of his car that had been held in safekeeping in her back pocket.

"Here, no you have it."

"Have what? What is all of this Alicia?"

"When I met Marilene this morning, I felt like she looked familiar to me. When I questioned her about it, she in a way was quite dismissive about it."

James raised his eyebrows and gave Alicia a glassy stare, "Where is all of this going Alicia?"

"After the meeting, I figured out where I might have known her from."

"And where might that be?"

"Now, I can't be one hundred percent certain but I think she's actually Scarlett Montgomery, she used to be married to Carson Montgomery, his parents are the pastors of Wondrous Works Tabernacle Fellowship in California; my mother is a member there."

Opening his mouth to criticize Alicia for her suspicions, James stopped short, "C'mon Alicia, this isn't like you. Why would you go through all of this?"

Alicia's face reddened, her posture was now taut, the cords in her neck twinged, "Look, I don't want to see you get hurt or better yet, made a fool of by putting all of your eggs in one basket with this woman. I don't trust her."

"Alicia, I appreciate your concern but even you have to admit these photos don't even look like her."

"James, I asked my mother about her and she told me that apparently, this Scarlett woman just up and left her husband. To keep down further embarrassment to the church and the family, they tried to erase anything related to her. Now that he's remarried, they have pictures of his new wife up in her place. The only thing is, my mother doesn't throw anything away and she had some old programs with her picture on them. I asked her to send them to me. I will say, you do have a point, the woman in these pictures don't look like her now but what if they did years ago? I searched all over the Internet looking for a Scarlett Montgomery and a Marilene Watson and I didn't find much on either name. This could be why she so needs to stay in the background and not be exposed. Who knows? All I know is, something is a little off with her and I don't like it."

Tapping the top of his car, "Alicia, this could be her and it could not be her, but no matter what happens, I believe everything is going to work out just fine. In the brief time I've known her, I've never questioned about her past because guess what, we all have one. What's happened in the past is just that, it's in the past. Now, I appreciate you looking out for me but I promise you, I'm good."

"Alright, I hear you. Please know I only have your best interest at heart here."

"Don't you know I already know that? Now, come give me a hug, I need to get going. Thanks for inviting me out this evening, I had a great time. We'll talk soon."

James couldn't wait to get into his car, "Okay, Lord I don't have time to walk tonight but you and I really need to talk. But first let me do this."

"Hey there Marilene, imma turn in early 2nite. Let's talk 2moro."

CHAPTER 33

"**I** think I have the Carson cooties."

"Let's be clear here, I will never be known as having cooties. But, why do you say that, you feeling okay?"

"I think I may be coming down with the bug you've been struggling with. I'm not feeling well at all babe."

Carson walked over from the bathroom and felt Rebekkah's forehead.

"You don't feel warm sweetie. What symptoms do you have?"

Rebekkah rolled away from Carson and grabbed her stomach. Everything on me hurts, my head, my stomach...you know that feeling where you just don't feel well? If you know what I mean, then that's what I feel like."

Rubbing his wife's back, a thought popped into Carson's head. The thought didn't last long in his head, he blurted it out through his mouth before his head could stop him, "Ah-ha, you're pregnant."

Rebekkah wanted to hide, she avoided eye contact with her husband and used the covers to shield herself from his excitement.

"No, no way. I'm not pregnant."

"How do you know, have you taken a test yet?"

"No, I haven't."

"Well then you don't know for sure. That would explain your recent moodiness and eating so much. Girl, you have really been packing it on. Yes. Finally. I'm going to be a father and oh yes, I will be praying it is a boy. Lord knows that would make me a happy man."

"Hey, hey, hey...you are getting way ahead of yourself Carson. You better watch it buddy, I haven't been moody and I don't eat too much."

"Uh and okay to not being moody. Listen, I hate to leave you like this but I need to get prepared for tomorrow's message. I have a full day planned because I figured you'd be at the luncheon today...oh no, the luncheon. Are you too sick to go?"

"Carson, I'm sick. Can't you see that I don't feel well? Your mother should understand that. Anytime anyone asks her about this event, all she can say is that she wants it to be perfect. I don't want my sickness to put a damper on her precious little luncheon."

Laying down beside Rebekkah, Carson turned Rebekkah towards him.

"Tell me the truth."

Rebekkah trembled on the inside.

"Are you feeling some sort of way because my mother started this luncheon with my ex?"

Rebekkah breathed out a sigh of relief, "Carson, while I don't particularly like having to step into the shoes that Scarlett left, I'm willing to do it if it means being married to you. Today, I just don't feel well. I'm sorry I have to miss it but there will be plenty more. I don't see where this one event will make or break me."

Carson kissed Rebekkah on her cheek, "Alright sweetie, I need to get going. I'm still not feeling my best either but I don't have time to be sick right now. The show must go on, right? Truly, there is no rest for the weary. Hey, would you like for me to call mother and let her know you won't be there today?"

Rebekkah smiled through her sickly looking face, "If you don't mind sweetheart, I'd really appreciate it."

"I'll check in with you later, I probably won't be back home until tonight. While I'm out I'm going to buy you a pregnancy test and we'll try it out later."

"That's fine, do what you need to do. I know how important both speaking tomorrow and having a baby are to you right now. I'm going to get some rest; you go on ahead. The quicker you leave now, the quicker you can come back to me tonight."

Minutes after Carson left, Rebekkah made sure the coast was clear and safe to leave. Her window of opportunity was short.

The car service she'd previously arranged pulled up outside of her home.

"If all goes well, I should be back before anyone notices I'm gone."

CHAPTER 34

"Good afternoon. Welcome ladies. It's so nice to see you again."

Hugging and greeting woman after woman during the welcoming reception, Regina Montgomery was working the room. She was being such a gracious hostess, offering hospitality and it was certainly without grumbling.

Impeccably dressed from head to toe, Regina represented the Montgomery family well on this special occasion.

The grounds of the Montgomery estate had been transformed to accommodate the annual luncheon.

The luncheon would be a time of fellowship, a time of refreshing, a time of ministry.

No one knew better than Regina how important it was to receive impartation while fulfilling the role of a pastor or minister's wife.

In some small way, she viewed this event as her way of giving back, her area of ministry outside of her husband.

As a veteran in the ministry, Regina knew how to speak to the very heart of wives who stand beside their husband's calling.

The air-conditioned tent housed over five hundred women who had come from near and far for the afternoon.

Shades of mauve and teal adorned the meeting space, the decorations were breathtaking.

The theme for the luncheon this year: "Extreme Makeover."

Mirrors hung from the draped ceilings, vanities topped with feminine and dainty items were strategically placed throughout the area.

In certain areas of the space, stations were set up with beauty experts waiting to grant actual makeovers to those who were brave enough.

Courtney walked up behind Regina, "Mama Montgomery, look who's here."

Regina turned around to see who Courtney was to reveal.

"Oh my Lord. Lucy, I can't believe you came all the way out here for this."

Lucy and Regina hugged while Courtney stood smiling from left to right.

"Well, I'm a first lady aren't I? Our families are soon to be tying the knot and there was no way I was going to miss such a wonderful time."

"Courtney didn't tell me anything about you coming. How were you able to keep this away from me girl? You will be staying with us while you're here, right?"

"When Courtney and Christian came home last week, they told me about what you were planning and I knew then I wouldn't miss it for the world. I even brought a few of my other first lady friends with me.

They are over there getting registered. We are all looking forward to having a high time in the Lord today, sister."

Regina pulled Courtney close to whisper in her ear, "The actual luncheon is to begin in fifteen minutes and Rebekkah isn't here, have you heard from her?"

"No ma'am, I haven't. I thought she was coming. Would you like for me to try and reach her?"

"Yes and tell her she needs to hurry up and get here."

The mistress of ceremonies started the program right on time with the first order of business, the invocation by Mother Betty Montgomery, a true soldier in the army of the Lord.

Make no mistake about it, her prayers didn't bounce off of the ceiling and come back down. You could feel her words touch the gates of heaven and expose you to all of its glory. The windows of heaven were now open above the prim and proper preacher's wives.

Mother Montgomery brought the house down with her anointed prayers, she summoned the All Mighty to be present in their midst and move in a special way. After hearing her pray, there was no question as to whether or not He was there...because He was.

The program continued as scheduled. Still no Rebekkah.

Regina was livid but she kept her cool. She had to. She was going to be speaking after the food service.

"Scarlett and I started this event years ago and I'm not going to let that ole Ratchet Rebekkah ruin this for me. I'll deal with her later. Scarlett, my dearest

Scarlett, I don't know where you are but this day is for you."

Regina hand selected every morsel served to her guests and by the empty plates, she had apparently done a remarkable job.

Everything was working like a well-oiled machine. The time for Regina to deliver the word was quickly approaching and Rebekkah was set to introduce her new mother-in-law.

Still no sign of Rebekkah.

Not having any luck reaching Rebekkah, Courtney quickly seized the opportunity to score more daughter-in-law points and she stepped in to introduce the speaker of the hour.

Regina graced the podium with refinement and pure elegance despite the disappointment she felt being stood up by the likes of Carson's new wife.

For the moment at hand, she shook off her offended feelings.

"I'm on an assignment today, I've been given a mandate to share something real with you ladies today."

Normally, Regina would have a long list of honorable mentions she'd go through but today was different. She went straight into her message.

"As you look around you, there are mirrors everywhere. I want you to find one, there should be one in front of you on your table. Look at it and look at yourself real good."

The ladies all took turns looking at themselves in their mirrors, showing off their good sides and having a good time.

"I see you all enjoyed that but let me ask you something. Do you like what you see? When your husband looks at you, does he like what he sees? Does your congregation like what they see when they look at you? Most importantly, what does God see when He looks at you?"

Women all over the room shifted in their seats. For some they were used to the patty cake messages Regina was known for, not the one she was about to deliver.

"Yes, ponder on the answers to those questions for a moment. If you're anything like me and you're honest with yourself, I'm certain there is at least one no in there somewhere."

Regina was fully assured of her mission, there wasn't anything or anyone who was going to stop her.

"I already know based on what the word tells me that only a percentage of you are going to fully hear and receive what I'm going to say but this word on my heart today is for all of us as first ladies if we'll heed to it."

Regina stood tall and squared her shoulders back, "This year's theme, Extreme Makeover, there once was a show with the same name. In this show, people would volunteer to undergo extensive changes in Hollywood. They would willingly subject themselves to radical procedures to change what they looked like on the outside."

Several women at their tables nodded their heads in agreement, voicing their acknowledgment, "Yes, I used to watch that show."

Regina walked with purpose as she strolled back and forth across the stage, establishing eye contact with every set of eyes she came across.

"I have another question for you. How many of you would be willing to submit to an extreme makeover, a radical departure from what you are accustomed to?"

Hands were raised all over the room, some clapped while some shouted their answer.

"Before you answer, let's go to our life line, let's see what the word has to say. Our scripture text will be coming from the entire third chapter of Colossians."

Once she read the scripture, Regina seemed to loosen up and settle into a good natured approach but not losing her assertiveness as she delivered what had been placed on her heart.

"Now, I know many of you took all morning long trying to make sure you looked right before coming here. I know you did it because I did."

Soft laughter filled the room.

"Often times in the position we serve as first ladies, we forget that we are to do just that, serve. Somewhere down the line, we have been led to believe that this life is all about the preferred seating, the big hats, the luxuries and the lime lights of this high calling. Listen here ladies, we are not here to become label whores, worried about who's wearing what."

Some listened while others were already turned off yet they couldn't really show it. Regina Montgomery was speaking for God's sake.

"Pick up those mirrors again. Look at yourself. What do you see? Please tell me you aren't like the scribes and the Pharisees in Matthew 23:27 where you look beautiful on the outside but your insides are full of dead men's bones and all sorts of uncleanliness.⁷"

Regina was going somewhere and many of those present were coming along for the ride.

"According to the scriptures, the only garment we should be concerned with and putting on is love. It's an all-purpose garment that we should never be seen without. It's time to stop worrying about being pretty and looking good and serving God's people."

Regina expounded upon her message going through the other articles of clothing, we as Christians should wear, the wardrobe hand-picked by God such as: compassion, kindness, humility, quiet strength and discipline. She admonished the women to climb down from their pedestals and serve the sheep God has entrusted to their flocks.

"When we look ourselves in the mirror, we should be striving to be a reflection of Jesus. When our husbands and congregations see us, they should be seeing a reflection of Christ. When Jesus looks at us, He should be seeing a reflection of Himself."

Breaking from her impassioned appeals, Regina surprised the crowd with a hidden talent and sang a few lines, "If I'm not mistaken, *Disney's Mulan* asks, "When will my reflection show, who I am inside."

Who knew? Regina's voice was beautiful.

"Tell me ladies, are you ready to allow His reflection to show through you?"

Regina started winding down and prepared to close.

"I know I've said a lot here today but I want you to understand that what ties us all together is love, for

---

[7] **Matthew 23:27**: *"Woe unto you, scribes and Pharisees, hypocrites! for ye are like unto whited sepulchres, which indeed appear beautiful outward, but are within full of dead men's bones, and of all uncleanness."*

without it, we are nothing. As the women who stand behind our husbands we need to have the Lord fill our hearts with a new dose of His love. I'm not saying, all will be well over night. We might struggle with this new way. However, with His love, we will change from the old and experience an extreme makeover from the inside out."

Regina closed her notes.

"If you are here today and this message has spoken to your heart and you want a fresh infilling of His love, meet me up here so we can touch and agree for your extreme makeover."

Scores of women came forward. The word been preached and it brought forth much needed healing and deliverance.

All of Regina's planning and hard work paid off, everyone could not stop talking about how much they'd been blessed. Every single detail had not gone unnoticed. From the physical makeovers to the delightful gift baskets they received as tokens from attending.

"Regina Montgomery, I'm here to tell you, you have outdone yourself with this luncheon here today. Wonderful. Awesome. Fabulous. Woman of God, I know your husband is proud of you. I am going back to my husband and my church with a renewed sense of ministry. Blessings upon you for all you have done in this place today."

These were just some of the words many of the women were leaving Regina with as they left to return to their respective places of worship.

CHAPTER 35

"Where are you?"

Rebekkah replied with high pitched laughter, "What do you mean silly? I'm home, in bed. Remember? Isn't that where you left me?"

Carson deepened his tone, "Oh yes; that is where I left you but you certainly aren't here now."

Rebekkah began speaking quickly and asking questions to figure out if she'd been busted.

"Honey, what's going on? Aren't you calling to check on me? Where are you right now?"

Carson's anger was on a simmer, set to start boiling and it would eventually explode.

"I see you think this is funny, you seem to think I'm in the mood to play games with you. Where are you and don't you lie to me."

Fearful of what the truth might bring, Rebekkah rattled off, "I stepped out to the store. I kept thinking about what you said, you know, that I might be pregnant. So, I came out to get something to eat and grab a pregnancy test."

Pinching his bottom lip, "If that's true, why is your car still here? How are you getting around?"

"I called a cab Carson, I didn't feel like driving."

Technically that part was true but she conveniently left out the details surrounding the cab ride.

Rebekkah arranged for a car service to pick her up and take her to a rental car appointment. When she arrived, the rental car was waiting for her to make the turn and burn to her sister's shower.

Carson made a hmmm noise in his throat, "How long before you get back home?"

"I haven't been gone that long, I should be home within the hour."

That too was technically the truth, she had not too long ago left the shower; she'd already been on the road for about an hour and a half.

Carson sat on the bed and tried to sort out his thoughts about the situation, "Alright then, I'll wait for you."

"No honey, there is no need for you to do that. What about all of the preparation you have to do for tomorrow?"

Carson did a quick mental rundown of everything he knew about the situation.

"Rebekkah, tomorrow will take care of itself. Right now, I'm more interested in you. Since you're getting the pregnancy test, come on home so we can see what it says. I'll be here waiting on you."

"Okay, if you insist. By the way, you never answered why you are at home."

"I left my phone this morning and I guess we are truly dependent upon these things. I tried to see if I could manage through the day without it but I couldn't. I needed it for too many things, my entire life is wrapped up in this little thing."

The conversation about the phone seemed to lighten the mood somewhat, until he said, "I have a bunch of missed calls from, looks like everybody. I guess I'll check in and see what's up while I wait for you to get here."

"So you didn't get a chance to tell your mom that I wouldn't be making the luncheon?"

"Did you not hear what I said? No, I told you I left my phone at home. I'm sure she figured it out."

"I hope she isn't too upset that I didn't make it today."

"You said you weren't feeling well, right? She'll just have to accept that. I know she'll accept it a lot more if it's because she's getting ready to have her first grandchild."

"And on that note, I'm going to let you go. I'll see you soon."

"Omigoodness, that was close. Gee whiz, now I need to stop and get a pregnancy test. What I need to do is call my ride in to meet me at the car rental place so I can get home."

Carson looked through his phone, looking to see who he would call first. *"I should probably call mama and let her know what happened."*

Before he could call, he received a text message from his brother-in-law with a picture attached:

"Thx so much 4 all of the baby gifts n the shower. U n big sis hooked us up, sis did her thing 2day, sorry u cldn't b here. Thx again brutha!"

There it was in living color, Rebekkah standing with her sister, Darla and her husband, Noah at their baby shower.

CHAPTER 36

"Look who's here, it's Ms. Hermit Crab in the flesh. I can't believe you have been inside that house and not gone anywhere since your parents left. Who does that?"

"The person who has no life. That's who and that person is me."

Scarlett waddled into James' home and went straight for the kitchen, "What are you cooking in here, it smells delicious."

While they had talked, James had not seen Scarlett since the day of the meeting and also the day Alicia confronted him about her.

"That person doesn't have to be you; I keep trying to get you to go out with me. Nevertheless, I'm glad you decided to come over and be neighborly and allow me the opportunity to cook for you and our little soccer player here."

In passing, James landed a delicate touch to her stomach acknowledging the baby's presence without being awkward. The baby noticed.

Nestled on one of the bar stools, Scarlett laughed, "I think he's grateful for the invitation."

James enjoyed spending time with Marilene or Scarlett or whoever she was. Trying to reconcile Alicia's suspicions against the magnetic attraction he felt towards her, he came up with the following conclusion. To him, for whatever reason, she had not yet felt comfortable sharing that part of her life and it was okay. At which point she was ready, he'd be there to hear it without judgment.

"A Cinderella for the princess." James remembered Scarlett ordering that at the restaurant and found the ingredients to make for her at his house.

The sparkly mocktail paired well with the spread of hors d'oeuvres James had out while he prepared his dinner menu.

There was something about watching James deglaze his skillet while wearing his "Emeril Is My Homeboy" apron that drew Scarlett in.

"You are having way too much fun here, what can I help you with?"

"Not a thing, just sit there and look pretty." James walked over with a spoon of his sauce for the roasted chicken. "You can taste this and tell me what you think."

Pretending to be blown away, Scarlett savored every bit of that sauce, "Is there no end to your awesomeness? That is yummy. I can't wait to taste the rest."

James smiled over his shoulder as he attended to the many dishes he was preparing, "There's more where that came from, you just wait and see. Not much longer now. I'm going to hurry up, you over there looking like you ready to eat."

Scarlett got up and asked for the restroom. She had pregnant lady problems, frequent trips to the bathroom were now a way of life.

On her way back to James, she took the liberty to walk around the open floor plan of his home and look around.

Looking at his pictures made her smile. The way he had them set up seemed to tell the story of his life. She noticed the pattern stopped after a picture of him standing with a very attractive woman at a movie premier.

"Hmmm, there must be a story here. I wonder what it is. Shoot, I have one too and I'm not ready to tell it so I better keep my mouth shut about his."

Giggling to herself about the thoughts going on in her head, James asked, "What's so funny? I thought I flushed the last time I was in there."

Scarlett howled in laughter, "You are so crazy. Nah, I was admiring your pictures and I thought the one of you as a little boy in the shorts suit with the knee high socks was simply adorable."

James started to prepare the dining room table for his feast, "Oh yeah, a brother like me been styling and profiling from the beginning. You can call me blue cheese because I'm always dressed."

James pulled out a chair for Scarlett, as they sat for dinner, he grabbed her hand and blessed their food and fellowship.

Scarlett could feel from his velvety smooth hands that he used his hands for good, for helping people.

"I think I may have figured you out."

"And what great mysteries have you uncovered my fair lady?"

"I can tell you enjoy taking care of people, don't you?"

In an ominous manner, James carefully removed his napkin from his lap, got up from the table, and started to walk away.

"Hey, where are you going with your crazy self?"

James turned around and moseyed his way back to the table stopping behind Scarlett's chair.

"You know my secret, I've been exposed and you know what happens when people learn about my secret...they aren't around to tell anyone else about it."

By this time, he'd made his way back in front of her. The two looked at each other and they both fell out laughing. Scarlett snorted. James cackled. The duo continued to laugh unto tears. The scene was hilarious; they became quite silly with one another.

The accidental touches they shared were comforting.

Truth was, Scarlett had figured James out. He grew up in a giving family, starting with his father, Derrick giving him his identity and changing his life for the better.

Throughout his life, he was always concerned about the welfare of others which shaped his desire to become a doctor. He received fulfillment by bringing happiness and satisfaction to others. Scarlett was now a part of his mission to make her life better. He gained energy from giving of himself.

The cool, coconut lime sorbet balanced the warm, chocolaty notes found in the moist made from scratch cake.

Scarlett could only close her eyes in response to the delightful dessert, "You're spoiling me, a girl could get used to this."

James tested the waters and stepped out of his comfort zone, "And I hope you do."

Scarlett's flushed cheeks signaled to James his charm was working even if she was trying to repress her intentions.

Scarlett tried to think of something witty or funny to say to deflect the direct flirtatious comment but she couldn't. Her thinking was now fuzzy.

For the first time in a long time, there was a force building up in her princess parts and it wasn't from the baby. Experiencing emotional connections with James that night was causing her body to respond with a strong reactive way. A way that she could not elude him to. So what was she to do?

"As always, tonight has been wonderful but I think it's time for me to head home."

"Why? George and Minta are out of town, you're getting ready to go home to an empty house. I was hoping you'd stay over and we have an old-fashioned sleep over. We can watch movies, pop popcorn, and stay up all night. Wasn't it you that said you have no life. It's the weekend. Please tell me what else do you have to do tonight?"

"Stay at his house? Is he crazy? I really don't want to go home but I think I need to go home and take a cold shower. Now I see why God wants us to be married when we have babies. The struggle is real."

"So you staying or not man? As you can see, I have plenty of room so you can sleep wherever you feel most comfortable. Plus, there is no way I'd do anything to you or let anything happen to you because I would not want

George, no let me clarify, I don't want no parts of Minta."

Scarlett sat thinking a little longer, an image of Minta chasing James down the street with a meat clever made her giggle.

"So, what's going to be the first movie we watch?"

CHAPTER 37

"Thank you for driving me home so fast sir. Here is a little something extra for your troubles."

Seeing the sizeable tip, "Oh it was no trouble at all ma'am. Anytime you need a ride, call me and I'll be right here for you. You need any help with your bags."

"No thank you. I'll be fine."

"I hope you have a real nice evening ma'am."

"You and me both, I hope so too. Thanks again."

Unsure of the climate inside the house, Rebekkah walked in slowly looking for any sign of Carson.

Not seeing him on the first floor, she carefully made her way up the winding staircase.

Their bedroom door was shut. She peered around the door to find Carson knocked out snoring on top of the covers.

"He's out like a light, he's been really tired lately. I don't know if I should let him sleep or let him know I'm here."

Tiptoeing across the room towards the bathroom, the bag with the pregnancy test in it slipped out of her hands, "Dang it."

Waking from his nap, Carson realized upon seeing his wife there wasn't enough sleep in the world to keep him from going off on her, yet he played it cool. Briefly.

"I see you made it back. Two hours later, I guess there was a long line at the pharmacy, huh?"

Rebekkah could tell by the tone in his voice something was wrong. He didn't sound the same from their previous conversation."

Carson sat on the edge of the bed watching Rebekkah with a glassy stare.

Not sure how to respond, Rebekkah tried to change the subject and offered to take the test, "You wanted me to pick this up, right? You want me to do it now?"

"I say, do it when you want to. Isn't it right that you do what you want to do anyway?"

Rebekkah closed the bathroom door behind her, she was grateful for the shield the door provided. Her heart began to beat inside of her ears. She trembled as she unwrapped the packaging. She sat down to pee but nothing. She had to run the water from the sink to try and see if she could get a trickle going.

"Don't you think we should be together when you see the results? I'd like to be near you when we find out I'm going to be a daddy."

Splashing the running water in her face to try and calm her nerves, Rebekkah yelled out, "I'll be right out honey."

Rebekkah sat next to Carson, "Here goes nothing; we have to wait about two minutes."

Those two minutes ticked away at a snail's pace. The couple didn't say a word to one another as they waited for the results.

Negative.

Catching sight of the result before Carson, Rebekkah broke down and started to cry, hoping to elicit some sympathy from her husband.

A heavy sigh and a bitter smile escaped from Carson's mouth, "So you're not pregnant."

"Not this time honey but we can keep trying." Rebekkah grabbed his hand.

Carson had played over and over in his mind how he was going to confront his wife but being in the moment, he still was unsure how he was going to react.

Releasing his hand from Rebekkah's, his stony expression crushed her.

"What's wrong honey, you're scaring me. Talk to me."

Carson struck out, he exploded, he lost all of his composure; "You want me to talk to you, huh? What should I talk about Rebekkah? Oh let's see, let's talk about how you lied to my face this morning pretending to be sick. Or maybe we should talk about how you purposefully defied my mother by not showing up at her luncheon today. Hey, I got one for you, let's talk about this lovely, family photo Noah sent me thanking for me for all that we did for them at their shower."

Rebekkah held her hands up in a defensive stance, speaking in a soothing pacifying voice, "Honey, calm down. I can explain."

Carson turned around and punched the nearest wall. He got up in Rebekkah's face and pointed his finger, spittle built up around the corners of his mouth. The nerves in his face began to twitch. He was a raging animal.

"Carson. Calm down, you're scaring me."

"There is no explanation for this. If you can explain this away then maybe you can help explain to me why after your little stunt, Bishop has decided that I won't be preaching tomorrow."

"What? Wait a minute, why did he decide that?"

"They are punishing me for your deception. I hope you didn't think you could pull a trick like this and challenge the leadership who also happen to be my parents and not receive any repercussions."

Rebekkah shook her head, "I'll call them. I'll apologize and explain my actions. They need to deal with me on this, not you."

"I believe Bishop's exact words were, if a man does not know how to manage his own household, how will he take care of the house of God?"

Carson squeezed his fists up in the air, "Rebekkah, do you have any idea, what you have done? I can't believe this is happening. My father is now questioning my ability to lead Wondrous Works. He's now reconsidering me as his successor all because you felt the need to attend a stupid baby shower? You have got to be freaking kidding me. I hope that shower was all you thought it would be."

Carson was speaking his mind, with no filter. He stooped to hurling insults that he knew would jab her below the belt.

"Do you know all I've done to make it to this point? I chose you to become the new Mrs. Montgomery because I convinced myself to believe you had what it took to help me lead this church. But now I see I was wrong, I was fooling myself. My wife, Scarlett, she had my back in this, you just had my front. I was bound by the sheets with you and stupid me, I couldn't get out before it was too late."

Rebekkah reacted calmly to the rebuke, however, she was trying to think of ways to deal with the possible fallout.

"Listen, I know you are upset but you don't have to be mean. We can work through this, if we work together."

"I'm not here to work out anything. You are the one that messed up, you better do whatever you can to show this church and me that you are in this for the long haul."

"Why did you stop? Sounds like you wanted to say, or else."

"Look, I'm not playing any games with you. I say what I need to say. I say what I mean and I mean what I say. But if you need to hear it, you better shape up or else..."

"Or else what?"

"You already know. Maybe you should ask Scarlett. Oh, that's right. You can't. No one can."

CHAPTER 38

"Good morning and thank you all for being here this morning. Time is really moving, can you all believe we are seven weeks away from the health fair? It's seems like we all were just here together a few days ago. Anyway, Alicia is running a little behind this morning. But maybe by the time we all go around and get status updates from everyone she'll be here."

James sat at the head of his conference room table and seated directly to his right was Scarlett.

"Before she goes, I just have to tell you guys that Marilene shared with me some of the emails and letters she's been receiving through her blog and man, it's enough to make a grown man cry. Her blog is touching the lives of so many people just by simply, walking and talking. I knew from the start when I heard about it that it was going to be a nice addition but I think we are blessed to be a part of what she is doing. I'm sorry, am I talking too much? Let me hush, go head girl, do your thing. Tell us what's up."

Scarlett sat up straight in her swivel chair, "I really don't have much to add to what James has already said. With the marketing support from the Calhoun's our analytics indicate more and more people are finding the site and they are actually signing up for the challenge and also registering for the health fair."

Alicia walked in while Scarlett was providing the group with her updates. Alicia walked in and wouldn't take her eyes off of Scarlett.

Scarlett continued on, "I love the pictures from the photo shoot with Raquel, I think she represents the campaign very well. Outside of that, that's all I have for today."

Everyone went around the room and gave their respective updates and it ended up with Alicia who was seated directly to the left of James. With these two women on each side, he was sitting between fire and ice.

James announced, "The floor is all yours Alicia, do you have anything new to report to us?"

"No, not really. Everything is going according to plan. We are on task and on budget."

"Is that it? Excuse me but who are you and what have you done with my planner, Alicia? Hey, you usually have more to say than that. Everything okay?"

Alicia shrugged her shoulders, "Yes, I'm fine. I mean hey, when you have a great team there isn't much to report on, right? Everyone is doing their job."

James figured Alicia still must have been harboring ill-will towards Scarlett with her suspicions but he was not willing to add any fuel to the fire with her. He was not going to pet her with that. It still didn't matter to him. Over the last month, he and Scarlett had continued to get to know one another and not one time had she mentioned it and he wasn't concerned about it either.

"Well, in that case, we can dismiss early and we all can go about our merry ways. Thanks again for showing up this morning. Seven more weeks guys. Grab some food before you leave, don't y'all leave me here with all of this food."

"Hey Alicia, Carlos is supposed to be stopping by, I told him we were meeting this morning and he wanted to finally go ahead and sign up to be a vendor. Would you happen to have the new vendor application ready for him to fill out? If not, we'll use the old one."

"So are you and Carlos now besties? I heard you guys have been hanging out without us girls, what's up with that?"

"I can't help it if I'm such a likeable guy. Those guys are some real cool dudes and I'm glad Carlos has decided to sign up."

Alicia pulled out the new form and looked up at the door, "Speak of the devil and he shall appear."

Carlos entered the conference room with the others. Despite being done early; no one was ready to leave. They were caught up in their own little side conversations.

"Good morning Alicia, you're looking rather beautiful this morning. We missed you at Lyla's house last night. I thought you were coming over."

"Yeah, I was but I ended up working late on another project I'm working on. I heard you all had a good time though."

"We did, but it wasn't the same without you."

"So you say. You're here to fill out the application right?"

"Yes. And to see you."

"Okay Casanova, I've heard enough. Sign this form so you can go."

Sarah and Scarlett were seated at the table talking about the baby when Minta called. Scarlett excused herself to answer her mother.

James noticed the disappointment in Scarlett's face upon her reentry into the room.

Walking over to her before she could sit down he said, "Hey, what's wrong, what happened?"

"Lord, I know Alicia hasn't said something to this girl about her crazy hunches."

"I'm fine James."

"Marilene, I can look at you and tell something is bothering you. C'mon tell me what's up."

Scarlett decided to tell him, "My mother just called to tell me she has an out of town consultation that can't be rescheduled and she leaves the day I'm supposed to start my child birth education classes."

Thinking nothing of it, "Girl. You had me worried. That's nothing, I'll go. Problem solved."

Scarlett stepped back, trying to put some distance between herself and James.

"I didn't tell you that for you to offer to come. You don't have to do this."

Stepping forward and closing the distance, James replied, "Why are you always telling me what I don't have to do? And I didn't offer for you to refuse woman. Look, I'm a doctor, why wouldn't you want to go with me? Who else are you going to go with, George? He just doesn't strike me as the type."

The thought of George in the child birth classes made them both laugh.

Scarlett pinched the bridge of her nose and squeezed her eyes shut, "Alright, alright, you win. How is that you always seem to talk me into doing stuff?"

"But have I steered you wrong though?"

"No, you have not."

"Well then, I see no issues here. When are we going to our first class?"

CHAPTER 39

"I was wondering how long it was going to take you to call. I guess having no lights will make you call people you don't want to talk to."

"Man, do you know how many times growing up our lights got cut off? I wasn't tripping about the lights, I just did what we did growing up, I lit some candles. I figured you must've been trying to prove a point so I decided to call."

"Well, I'm sorry I had to go to such extremes Travis but I'm glad you called. Your lights will be turned back on today."

"What do you want?"

"Travis, I haven't seen or heard from you in over a month. You and I need to talk."

"I think I was pretty clear the last time I saw you. There's nothing for us to talk about if you aren't willing to tell your family about what's going on."

Travis was emotionally fragile when it came to George but he maintained his position and didn't offer George any wiggle room.

"You know what I see going on Travis? I see that you don't seem to care how they are going to react to the news about you and I and what's going on here. All you seem to care about is what you want and how you think it should go."

Travis was tired of dancing around George's feelings, he didn't care anymore about his acceptance; he felt it was time to show him how he really felt.

Travis went ballistic, yelling through the phone, "If you think that then you haven't learned anything about me at all. Ever since you came into my life, I've only wanted you. I missed not having you around. You think I want to hurt them? How about you think for a moment the hurt I feel, the hurt I've felt. You think I want to live like this? I shouldn't have to be sneaking around trying to meet up with you. Your wife, your kids, they deserve to know. I tried to make it simple for you so you didn't have to choose but you won't leave me alone. You keep trying to get me to come around and talk to you and right now, I'm all talked out."

The silence on the phone seemed louder than Travis' rants.

George thought long and hard before he spoke.

"Travis, I'm sorry. You're right. It's time I told them. We can't keep going on like this. The sooner I tell them the better off we all will be."

Travis began to weep at the thought of being able to come from out of the shadows of shame.

"Travis, I'm going to suggest a family barbeque and I want you to come over. I'll tell everyone then, okay? How does that sound to you?"

"When are you planning to have the barbeque?"

"Does next Saturday work well for you? I need to be able to give Cole enough time to be able to make it home for the weekend."

"Alright, I'll be there. You have no idea how much this means to me. Thank you."

"If this is what you need then hopefully it'll help you out. I love you Travis."

"I love you too George."

CHAPTER 40

"**D**on't you dare laugh, I know I look like an idiot."

Scarlett could not contain her laughter as she wobbled behind James carrying multiple pillows, blankets, the yoga mats, and a cooler filled with drinks and snacks.

"I told you not to bring all of that stuff but no you wouldn't listen to me. Let me help you carry something."

"No, I got it. You just keep walking."

Scarlett laughed all the way into the room. Her laughter waned once she stepped inside and saw all of the married couples there together for the class.

Being the attentive guy he was, James picked up on her feelings of disparity.

He mouthed under his breath, "Just go along with whatever they say. Play along okay. No one knows us here, we can be whoever we need to be."

"Welcome, Mr. and Mrs. Watson, is it?"

James answered quickly, "Yes ma'am, we are the Watsons and we are so happy to be here."

"Oh how delightful, I'm Emma and I'll be your instructor for this class. Here's your packet, feel free to find a space on the floor to settle in and we'll begin shortly."

James helped Scarlett down to the floor onto their mats and propped her up on the massive amount of pillows he bought. Nestling down behind her, securing his spot as her support he leaned in with excitement, "This a really good hospital, I'm glad you chose it. Over here, no one knows who I am so I get to pretend to be Mr. Watson tonight girl."

Scarlett felt at ease with James, he was always so funny and attentive.

"That makes two of us, no one knows who I am either. But, I'm not going to think about that tonight. I'm going to try and enjoy myself."

"Welcome again all of you soon to be mommies and daddies, we are delighted to have you join us for the first night of childbirth education. Our classes have been designed to in some small way prepare you for what is ahead in your journey towards labor and delivery. Giving birth is like a marathon. There are some things you have to do in order to prepare to run. You wouldn't just up and run a marathon without proper preparation would you? So why would you up and decide to go through childbirth without the right preparation?"

The teacher for the class was quite passionate about her job, you could tell she loved what she did. Maybe even a little too much.

"I look forward to spending the next four weeks together as we discuss every topic related to giving birth as our goal here is to empower you to make the best decisions about your delivery and reduce those pesky little jitters you might be having. And that goes for both mommy and daddy. We'll also talk about common childbirth complications, some potential post-partum issues, and breastfeeding."

The couple next to James and Scarlett leaned over and whispered, "Talk about loving your job. I get the sense she's going to try and teach us everything she knows. Lord, help us all."

James and Scarlett traded smiles with the future parents.

Emma was about to show the first video but held off for a moment, "Before we begin, I'd like for everyone to go around and introduce themselves. Each week, we'll take turns introducing but tonight, I want the husbands to do the introductions. Tell us who you are, what you're having, if you know, and one thing about your wife that makes you smile."

Scarlett's shoulders curled over her chest, she felt a piercing pain in the back of her neck. The charade was already proving to be too much for her, *"I knew this was a bad idea."*

She bargained and prayed, *"Lord, just help me to get through this first class. If I don't make it back at least I'll have some sort of understanding and I can look up the rest on the Internet."*

By playing a game of mental ping-pong with her thoughts and fears, Scarlett was surprised it was time for their introduction.

James stood up and straightened out his double-pleated slacks, he stood above the others like a high-rise apartment, there were definitely many levels to this man.

"Good evening everyone, my name is James Watson and this lovely lady seated here is my gorgeous wife,

Marilene Watson and it gives me great pleasure to announce we are expecting our first son."

James lunged forward and flexed his muscles. He garnered cackles from the crowd.

Kneeling down beside Scarlett, he took her hand in his and locked eyes with her. In that moment, he and Scarlett were the only two present.

"The one thing about this woman that makes me smile, is seeing her smile. When she smiles, I smile. I love every opportunity I have to make her smile."

All of the women in the group clutched their hearts and swooned.

Scarlett was beside herself, her heart was overwhelmed, her eyes sparkled with adoration.

Emma stood to start the video, a video showing the differences between a vaginal birth and that of a cesarean section.

"That was beautiful. Mrs. Watson, you are one lucky lady."

Scarlett blushed.

The video started.

The guy next to them passed out upon watching.

Emma quickly stood up, "Like clockwork, I think it's time we have our first break."

Without delay, James switched out from being the doting husband to the doctor he really was.

Emma rushed over with smelling salts, "This happens every class, last week we had three dads to pass out."

With a weakened voice, the not so tough guy spoke up, "Thanks man, I don't know what happened over there. I sure hope this doesn't happen in the delivery room. Dianah would never let me live that down. I'm Liam by the way."

James extended his hand, "No sweat man, it's all good. It happens to the best of us. I'm James."

"Yeah, James...I remember, the one who put all us guys to shame with that introduction of yours. I'm not going to be able to live that down either. I'm just glad next week is her turn."

The two men were forming an instant friendship when their budding ladies walked over to meet them with snacks and drinks in hand.

Scarlett interrupted them, "Sorry it took us so long to come back, I'm sure you can imagine there was a long line in the ladies room."

Dianah surveyed the room, cliques were forming during the break; she peeked over her shoulder and then leaned in to reveal a secret to their new favorite couple.

"James, your introduction was so touching, I hope and pray I find a man that looks at me like you look at Marilene."

Both Scarlett and James stuck their necks out and asked with hesitations, "Huh, what are you talking about? What about my man, Liam here?"

Liam smiled, "We're not married...just call us the Pretenders."

Dianah felt the need to explain further, "Things didn't go well with my daughter's father and I've decided to raise her without him. My best friend, Liam here decided he wasn't going to let me do that. He convinced me that it takes a village to raise a child and he's been here with me every step of the way. It was his idea to pretend we were married."

Dianah took a sip from her drink, "I hope I didn't turn you guys off from telling you all of my business in like the first five minutes of meeting you but from what I can tell, you guys are the coolest couple in here. I felt like I could share that with you two."

Scarlett looked up at James, "Should I tell them or should you?"

"Only if you want to my dear."

Scarlett leaned in closer, "We aren't married either."

The foursome all erupted in laughter. It had been established, they were instant friends bounded together by pretense.

Emma stood in the center of the room, clapping her hands together, calling attention, "Sounds like we are having way too much fun, break time is over. Let's begin again with our next video, shall we?"

CHAPTER 41

"Hi honey, how's my baby? They better be treating you alright in there, are they son?"

"Mom, we go through this every time, I'm fine. I'm not a baby anymore and yes, they are treating me well."

Seeing her youngest son incarcerated always weighed heavily on Regina to the point of tears but not to the place where she would miss his monthly video chats.

Video chats in prison? Yes, Cayden-James' prison camp was for those fortunate to have deep pockets which allowed for benefits not seen at other facilities.

"It's good to see you son. I see you cut your hair and I see that five o'clock shadow you have going on there."

"Yeah dad, I'm trying out a little something new, something different."

"Your mother and I are planning to come for visit as soon as we get your brother married off."

Regina jumped in, "Don't get me wrong, I'm thankful we get to see you on these calls but I need to lay eyes on my baby...oops, I'm sorry, I can't call you my baby anymore."

"That's right, their wedding is coming up huh? Speaking of those two, where are they? Is it just going to be us today? I don't see Carson or Rebekkah either."

"Courtney and Christian should be here any moment they went out to run a quick errand but promised they'd be back in time for your call. Carson on the other hand, he's probably not going to make it over here."

Normally the whole family gathered to have the time with Cayden-James but not this time.

"What's up with Carson? Is he alright? I haven't heard from that guy in a minute."

Bishop shook his head and lowered his voice, "I'm not sure what's going on with Carson. He's been having a rough time lately. Problems at home and he's been being sick a lot."

"Sick like how? I've never known him to be sick, I don't think I've ever seen him sneeze before."

"He's losing too much weight if you ask me. As his mother, I can look at him and tell something isn't right but he keeps insisting on dismissing me saying I'm worrying too much."

"He was up in my office the other day, we were talking about some plans for the church and his nose started to bleed. I panicked but he didn't seem surprised. When I asked him about it, he told me that wasn't his first one."

"Nowadays he's always tired. One day he's up and the next day, he says he feels like he's coming down with the flu or a cold. I don't know, that wife of his is probably beating him in his sleep."

"Mom. Why would you say something like that?"

"I'm only saying what I'm saying."

Bishop and Cayden-James both laughed and said, "Okay, and whatever that means."

Regina and the Bishop hated seeing Cayden-James in his predicament but seeing the dimples dance in his cheeks made it easier for them to accept he was managing as best as he could.

"Mom, dad...I'm sure I'll spend the rest of my life apologizing to you about what I did. I hope and pray you guys know how profoundly sorrowful I am."

Bishop grabbed Regina's hand, "We know son. You are paying your debt to society and you have repented before the Lord and that's all we can ask for. According to 1 John 1:9; if we confess our sins, God is faithful and just to forgive us and also to cleanse us from all unrighteousness. You've done that and if God has forgiven you, certainly we can. We love you son and we're praying for you."

Cayden-James stared down at his hands, his eyes began to water.

"I hear you dad. I mean, you're right. I have done those things, confessed...repented but I'm having a hard time forgiving myself. I made a huge mess of things. I messed up big time, some people lost their livelihoods because of me."

Bishop scratched his eyebrow, "Hey now, you listen to me, if you're struggling with forgiving yourself; you didn't hear a thing I preached as you were growing up. I don't think you understand the full magnitude of what the grace message is all about."

Regina saw her son was suffering, burdened by his own guilt and condemnation. She took over.

"Sweetheart, what your father is trying to tell you is that, what Christ did for us covers our past, present, and future sins. We can't take back what He did so we may as well accept it. If He says He's removed our transgressions as far as the east is from the west, why are you trying to bring them back home to yourself?"

Cayden-James rested his prickly bearded face in his hands.

"We're here for you son. We're going to go ahead and pray, I'm not sure what has happened to Christian and Courtney. I'm sure he'll catch up with you soon. He told me he put some money on your account yesterday and your mother and I sent our usual as well."

"I really appreciate you guys hanging in here with me. It's hard to believe I've already been in here almost two years. I'm hopeful about the appeal because I don't want to spend another three years here but if the appeal is denied, I'll do what I have to do to make it through."

CHAPTER 42

"You do realize we are probably missing my brother's call, don't you?"

"Yes baby but come on, we really need to talk about this. You and I need to make sure we are in agreement. It's not going to work if we aren't on one accord."

Courtney stopped her car at the park down the road from the Montgomery estate, hoping to convince her fiancé that it was time for them to strike.

Courtney and Christian sat down at the nearest park bench. While he knew Courtney had a point, his mind was on getting the chance to speak with his brother during his call.

Growing up, none of the boys were particularly close, they each were just so different, it was hard for them to find any common ground. The common ground they did have, which was the church, meant different things to each of them.

Nevertheless, Cayden-James and Christian had become extremely close throughout Cayden-James' trials and tribulations. Christian had become an outspoken supporter of his brother and was using his law school connections to find grounds for an appeal.

"Listen to me baby, you and I both know Carson and Rebekkah are spiraling out of control. Something is wrong with him but when I asked Rebekkah about it the other day she said he's refusing to go to the doctor. He keeps telling her whatever is wrong with him will pass but the truth is, it hasn't. She told me he hasn't been feeling well for a while."

Christian stared emotionlessly hearing the news about his brother, "Well you know I barely talk to that clown so I don't know what's going on with him. That dude is only out for himself. Do you know he hasn't checked on Cayden-James in over two months? You know I had issue with the way he handled himself after Scarlett left. I'm telling you Courtney, there is more to that story than what Carson tried to tell us. I'd be willing to put money on it."

Being cynical, Courtney scoffed thinking back to the day they were on the tennis courts with Rebekkah and Carson, "Oh but remember, we are men and women of the cloth, we don't place wagers."

The two lovebirds doubled over each other laughing.

"Okay now, hear me out. We will be getting married around the same time Bishop is supposedly retiring. Ever since Rebekkah missed the luncheon, Carson's list of duties and responsibilities at the church has been dwindling. On any day, we already appear more stable than them."

Christian responded with, "And to you that means, you and I should try and make a play for the church? Instead of Carson and Rebekkah taking over, you think it should be you and me?"

Playing on Christian's emotions and using Cayden-James to do it, "Baby, if he won't even see about his own brother, what kind of a pastor is he going to be to the members at Wondrous Works? But, see you, you care about your brother. You're always checking in on him. With my background and yours, we can take this church to another level."

Christian tossed a twig to the ground and checked his watch.

"Babe, I'm ready to go, we can talk about this later."

Courtney rubbed Christian in a way that got his attention, he was back under her command.

"Baby, those two are self-destructing. It's only a matter of time. Although, Rebekkah signed her own warrant when she missed that luncheon but I was right there to take her place. If we play this right, we will be able to step right in and take both of their places. I overheard your parents talking and your dad is not sure Carson is the right choice anymore."

Christian sat back and closed his eyes, "And how do you suggest we go about this master plan for world domination Courtney?"

Courtney brought to light her campaign for their covert operations.

"Babe, I see you've really thought about this."

"We can do this baby, it's ours for the taking. So, are we in?"

CHAPTER 43

"**I**f you guys don't hurry up, you're all going to be late."

From the moment George mentioned to Minta about having Cole come home for a family barbeque, Minta went into high gear planning. In order for her plans to come together, everyone would need to be out of the house. She'd made appointments for a full day of pampering at the spa for Scarlett and George and Cole would enjoy a day of golf up at the club.

"Scarlett, do you need me to help you get out of here on time?"

"No mama, um you seem to forget I'm thirty-four weeks pregnant. I'm moving as fast as I can."

Minta squealed, jumping up and down, "I know and I'm so excited. The countdown is on; he'll be here in a few short weeks. Another reason for you to get going so you can go and relax today. Once he gets here things will be much different."

George and Cole got ready to leave and Cole stopped by the guest room before he left. To Cole, a family barbeque would be the perfect time to introduce the girlfriend no one knew he had, Miss Marissa Coleman.

"Good morning beautiful. Did you sleep okay last night? I missed not being able to sleep next to you, I'm glad we are only here for the weekend."

Marissa beckoned for Cole to come closer to her as she sat working on her laptop, "Well hello there. I've been going crazy in this room all by myself. You know me, I'm always up early but I didn't know when would be a good time to come out. So, I started working on some of my assignments for class."

Cole reached in for a good morning kiss.

"I did sleep well though; this bed is amazing. Are you and your dad getting ready to leave?"

Cole could not take his eyes off of Marissa, to him, he thought she was the prettiest flower in the garden and she had been plucked out just for him.

"Yes, my mother is going crazy, trying to hurry us all out of the house but I had to come in here and see you before I left. I wanted to make sure you were really going to be alright being left here with my mom while we go to the course?"

Marissa put down her work and joked around a bit with her beau, "Go and have a good time, I'm sure I'll be fine. Although, I keep thinking back to the look on your parent's face, especially your mother's when we got here last night. Everyone was so surprised; I wish you hadn't sprung me on them like that. Anyway, today should be fine, I look forward to being able to spend some time with her. She can get to know me and likewise, I'd like to get to know her."

Cole lifted Marissa up from the desk where she was working and grabbed her by the waist, "I needed them to see in person, the woman I intend to spend the rest of my life with and I would've never been able to adequately express how I feel about you over the phone to them. So here we are. All of us."

Cole and Marissa had been dating for close to a year now. They'd met at the library. Cole, in his last year of graduate school and Marissa in her first. Cole was charting a path to follow in George's footsteps, only Cole was on a faster track than George. Despite wanting to major in business and go into banking like his father, Cole was a talented and gifted artist. His entrepreneurial efforts throughout college garnered him enough capital to invest. Receiving such wise counsel from George, his investments were substantial enough to acquire his own bank. It was a small one but a bank nonetheless.

Marissa, a nurse practitioner was in the second stage of her educational pursuits. Her ultimate destination was to become a Certified Nurse Midwife and open her own practice. Within her family, she'd witnessed several family members suffer from infertility and she took on a mission to learning more about what she could do to change the outlook of women's health.

Cole's hand rubbed up against Marissa's stomach, she gushed with pride; "You better get going before it's too late."

Cole planted a kiss on Marissa's succulent lips, "I love you. Keep your phone close. I'm sure I'll be bugging you all day seeing how things are going."

"I love you too, now go. I'll see you later."

With Cole's surprise guest for the weekend, Minta had not been able to plan anything for Marissa.

However, Minta figured she could use the help from her son's lady love in order to pull off a surprise of her own.

Minta and Marissa would spend the day preparing and getting to know one another.

CHAPTER 44

"**M**rs. Watson, I've called everyone on this list into the security gate like you asked me to."

"Thank you Marissa and I've told you to call me Minta, it's perfectly alright."

Marissa put the finishing touches on the decorations Minta had placed her in charge of.

"Everyone should be arriving soon; I couldn't have done any of this without Marissa. Thank you my dear. You know, I can see why my son likes you."

Marissa accepted her praise but offered some praise of her own, "You have done a fabulous job here, are you sure no one knows what you've been planning?"

Minta danced a little jig, "Not at all and that George, boy...is he ever so nosey. Let's just say, this weekend is all about surprises."

Peering down her nose at Marissa, "Starting with you missy."

Marissa grabbed at her temples on her head saying, "I know, I know, I can't believe Cole brought me here without y'all knowing."

"Minta lightly touched Marissa's forearm, "I'm only messing with you honey, you are a delightful surprise. You are welcome here anytime. You hear me? Now let's get cleaned up before our guests start to arrive."

"Yes ma'am."

Minta flew out of the shower to answer George's jibber-jabber, "Minta, what in God's name is going on out there? I thought we were supposed to be having a small, family barbecue and from the looks of it, it looks like a -."

"Surprise. Yes, you are right. We are having a surprise baby shower for Scarlett this evening. When you mentioned the barbecue, my mind went into overdrive and I thought, what better time than this to celebrate the pending arrival of our grandson."

Rushing his speech, "Minta, you should've told me. I, I had a different idea about how today was supposed to go and now you have made this be about you."

Minta spoke without thought, "Made this be about me? George, please tell me how celebrating our daughter's entrance into motherhood is about me? The sun on that golf course has apparently baked your brain. I suggest you get yourself a shower and cool off a bit before the party starts. Tonight is still about family; that was your focus, right?"

Through his tension-filled facial expressions, George managed to mutter a defeated, "Yes, family...that is the focus."

Minta placed her gold, beaded sandals onto her perfectly manicured feet.

"I'm going downstairs now; I'll see you when you come down."

Minta walked downstairs to find Marissa and Cole admiring the décor of the shower. Watching them, she beamed with joy at the way everything turned out. The blends of chocolate brown, greens, and blues matched well with the outdoorsy look she was going for. Scarlett would be so surprised.

"I see you guys beat me downstairs."

Marissa quickly answered, "Yes ma'am. I'm so excited, I don't want to miss a thing so I tried to hurry up and get back down here."

"Mom, you have outdone yourself in here today. Everything looks great and I love the theme."

"Cole, you were too young to probably remember this but as a little girl, Scarlett always wanted to go camping but she never got the chance to go. She signed up for girl scouts just so she could go on their annual camping trip and the weekend of the trip she was too sick to make it. She dropped out the next week. By the time you came along and wanted to go camping, she had no interest in camping with you, her baby brother."

"That's sounds like Scarlett."

"So when I was thinking about possible themes for the shower, I fell in love with this one. Having a little boy, she's probably going to be doing her fair share of camping."

The doorbell rang, breaking up the friendly banter.

The first guest to arrive. Dr. James Hartgrove.

Minta welcomed James into her home, "Oh my goodness, did you buy everything on the registry?"

James struggled getting into the doorway with all of his gifts, "I tried."

Minta helped him in, "James, I want to thank you for helping me out with the invites; I really appreciated it. We don't know many people here at all but I wanted to have some people here today to help us celebrate."

"Minta, I wouldn't have missed this for the world and I'd like to think those who have met your daughter feel the same way."

"Thanks for saying that James. Very well then, I have some people I'd like you to meet."

Minta escorted James into the family room to introduce him to Cole and Marissa.

"Cole and Marissa, this is a good friend of the family, Dr. James Hartgrove. He and Marilene have been working together, preparing for his upcoming health fair where her blog will be featured."

Marissa wondered aloud, "I thought your sister's -."

Cole pulled Marissa close, pinching her side in an effort to shut off her thoughts that had become verbal.

Minta intervened and suggested James place his gifts at the gift table.

James chuckled as he saw the table, Minta's interpretation of a gift table was a tent with lanterns and pine cone garnishes.

"Minta, you have transformed your home into a camping oasis. This is very nice."

More and more guests started to arrive. Liam and Dianah from class were in attendance along with James' staff and everyone involved with the expo, including Alicia.

George had not made it downstairs yet. He was frantically trying to get in touch with Travis. With every attempt, he was met with Travis' outgoing voice message.

"Travis, it's me. I need to talk to you. Call me when you get this message."

Thinking that George might be trying to back out, Travis was purposely missing his calls. He was not going to give him an opportunity to cancel. He'd go along with the original plan and show up at the family get together.

Minta came up to check on her husband. As she made it to their bedroom door, George bumped into her.

"George, are you alright? I was coming to check on you and you just walked into me like you didn't even see me."

"Minta, I'm ready now, please let's just go downstairs and try to make the best out of this situation."

Minta pulled back, "Situation? What about any of this is a situation George? You've been acting strange ever since you got home and found out about the shower. Is there something I should be aware of?"

George stood in silence for a moment.

"Minta, you've put a lot into this event. C'mon and let's go enjoy it."

George reached for her hand.

The doorbell rang out again.

Marissa answered the door as the unofficial hostess of the shower.

"Uh, yeah. Um, hi, I'm Travis. George invited me."

Not knowing the difference, Marissa welcomed Travis into the home with warm hospitality.

George and Minta were walking down the stairs holding hands and noticed Travis following Marissa into the party area.

CHAPTER 45

"**I**'ve been calling for the last hour. Why didn't you answer or call me back?"

"I wasn't in a place where I could answer or return your call. I figured, I'd be seeing you soon enough, we could talk then."

George had managed to get Travis out to the pool area alone. It was nice out there too. Minta had done a fine job, she had fire pits set up throughout the space. From the looks of it with the s'mores bars set up, everyone would at some point during the shower, would come out and enjoy building and roasting their own s'mores.

"Nice place you have here George. Are you trying to pull one over on me? I thought you said you were going to tell your family at a small barbecue, not at the baby shower of the century. What's going on here man?"

Travis was getting agitated.

"Calm down. My wife planned this shower without me knowing. It's a surprise for my daughter. I told you this was not the best time for me to be laying this on them but no, you had to have things your way and back me into a corner."

Unsure of who the guy was talking to his dad, Cole stepped outside to investigate the fireside chat they were having.

"Hey dad, who's this?"

George regained his composure, "Oh, hey Cole. This here is um, Travis. Travis, this is my son, Cole."

"Nice to meet you man."

"Same here Travis. Dad, mom just got a text from the front gate saying Scarlett is in the neighborhood. We should probably go inside and be ready for when she gets here."

"Sure thing Cole, we're right behind you."

George held Travis back for a second, "Don't go anywhere. We will resolve this tonight. No matter how long it takes."

"Surprise."

Everyone in the house cheered and applauded the guest of honor as she tried to collect herself from the baby shower bombshell.

In talking with Travis, George had missed the surprise and Minta noticed.

"Who is this boy with George? I didn't invite him and why would George allow him to miss seeing Scarlett walk through the door?"

Wanting to make sure she wasn't too startled, James walked over to the honoree.

Giving her a hug, "I hope we didn't scare you too much."

"Not too much. I was already on alert when I pulled up and saw the cars but what gave it away was when the next door neighbors stopped me on the way in as they were leaving and was like, congratulations, sorry we couldn't make it over tonight but we'll get the gift over to you tomorrow."

James shook his head, "I hope you don't share that tidbit with your mother. The neighbors might be banned from all future Watson soirees."

James was mesmerized by her.

"You look gorgeous. How did you enjoy the spa?"

"Thanks, the spa was everything. At the time, I had no idea my mommy makeover was for my surprise shower."

Minta overheard her daughter's comments and eased up beside her, "Were you really surprised? You look beautiful. It was so hard keeping this from you but I did it."

Winking at James, she answered, "Yes, mama I was surprised. Thank you for doing this, everything is so stinking cute."

"I see James has cornered you off to himself. Y'all come on over and let's get ready to eat. Plus, honey you have guests that are waiting to say hello."

For the rest of the evening, the guests enjoyed a bountiful, catered spread of campfire delights, played games, and opened presents.

Towards the end, Minta requested for everyone to come out and make s'mores, just like George imagined.

The s'mores bars were a huge hit. In fact, the entire shower was a hit, everyone was having a great time. With one exception. Travis. He was like a fish on dry land.

The shower seemed to take forever, he wanted it to be over so George could tell them the truth.

He was beyond excited when the party started to wind down and their guests started to leave.

It was about to be his turn; he was originally supposed to be the honoree but things got a little mixed up. It was fine though because all was about to be revealed.

CHAPTER 46

"Cole, that was the best baby shower I have ever been to. Your mother rocks. I will need to put her on our planning committee."

"Well, for all of the assistance you provided her with today, I'd say you have sown into good ground. You two transformed this place in hours. It made me happy to see my sister happy. She's been through a lot and I was so glad to be able to see her enjoy herself for a minute."

"Well, call me crazy but I think the source of her happiness comes in the form of a handsome doctor."

"I think you might be right about that. He does seem to make her smile. Hey, do you think we should still tell the family tonight?"

Cole and Marissa were off talking while Scarlett and James had struck up a conversation with Travis. Minta had taken a phone call and George was waiting inside for her.

"So, the shower was nice. I take it you're having a boy?"

"Yes Travis, the shower was nice and you are correct, I'm having a boy."

"Do you have any names picked out yet?"

Scarlett sat still in a noncommittal way, she didn't know this man; she wasn't so willing to share such intimate details about the name of her unborn child.

Truth was, she'd been putting it off but sooner or later she'd have to come up with something.

"I've tossed around a few things but I think I'd like to wait and meet him first before I name him something that'll brand him for the rest of his life."

The flames from the fire pits were keeping them all warm from the coolness of the springtide air. Those who remained had no idea it was about to get hot out there.

If George had his way, he would only tell his wife and children the news but seeing as though they had people there with him, he didn't want to prolong the inevitable any longer.

"Hey guys, I need to have your attention for a moment."

Everyone turned to look at George.

"What's up pops, what's on your mind?"

George began to speak but he was not his normally articulate self, he was rambling on about things that didn't seem to make sense.

"I have something I need to tell you guys and there is no easy way to say it."

Minta cut in on George, "Honey, this sounds serious and we still have guests here, do you think you should be sharing this information in front of people we don't know?"

"People like who, Minta?"

"People like this young man over here that no one has taken the time to introduce me to in my own house.

I met everyone here tonight but him and I keep wondering why that is?"

Travis stood up, "I know you aren't going to talk about me like I'm not even here?"

Cole stood up, "Hey guy, I think you might want to fall back on this one."

Minta blared out, "Excuse me, I don't know who you think you are."

Scarlett, barely able to lift herself from the pool lounger stood up, "Hey, what's going on here?"

James hopped up admonishing her to calm down.

Playing the referee, George demanded everyone to shut up and sit down.

"No one and I mean no one is to say another word until I'm done saying what I need to say."

Those standing obliged George's request.

"As I was saying, there is no easy way to say this but it needs to be said."

Minta sat with her arms folded across her chest, her leg shook with great agitation.

"I met Travis a year and a half ago. Before I retired and we moved here, Travis came into my life."

"What do you mean came into your life? A year and a half ago and we are just now hearing about him?"

"Minta, sit down. I said not another word."

"I had just graduated and was about to move away to my first job at a bank and I met a young woman by the name of Nadine Raulerson. She and I shared a brief stint together before I left Mississippi. I told her I would get in touch with her after I relocated. When I tried to call the number I had for her, I was told she'd moved away with no forwarding information."

Cole inquired of his father, "What are you trying to tell us dad?"

Everyone was sitting on the edge of their seats waiting to hear George's news.

"One day at work, I received a telephone call...a call that would forever change my life."

George began to tear up a little.

"The caller on the other end said, George Watson, my name is Travis Raulerson, you might have known my mother Nadine Raulerson and I think you might be my father."

Everyone gasped for air.

"Needless to say, I couldn't believe what I was hearing but I couldn't deny I knew her and that we'd been together so it could have been true."

Travis chimed in, "My mother died two years ago. I happened to be going through some of her things and I noticed she had two birth records for me. I had never seen one of the birth certificates and that one had George Watson's name listed as my father."

"Travis, I said no one is to say anything until I'm done."

"Shortly after his call, I flew here to Mississippi where Travis and I submitted DNA samples to establish paternity. What I wanted to get you all here today for was to tell you that Travis is my son."

A hush fell over the group.

George continued, "I didn't know how to deal with this information so I tried to keep things separate but that didn't work out so well. The reason I chose to retire here was so that I could establish a relationship with my son. He deserves to be a part of our family and our family deserves to know he exists."

George had finally done it, he'd told his family about Travis and Travis could not have been happier.

No one knew how to respond, Scarlett asked James to help her up, she pulled him by the hand and said, "I can't deal with this right now, get me out of here."

Cole and Marissa walked out without saying a word.

Minta stood looking at both George and Travis with tears streaming down her face.

She could take it no longer, she went for it, Minta pushed George into the pool and stomped off leaving him alone with Travis.

Trying to be serious but smiling on the inside, Travis scurried to the pool house trying to find George a towel and a change of clothes.

CHAPTER 47

"Who knew s'mores and secrets would be the theme for my baby shower?"

James made Scarlett comfortable on his sofa in his family room.

"Can I get you anything?"

"No James, I'm fine. I'm not tripping that my dad has a son but what is bothering me is that he kept this secret for so long from my mother."

James tried to make sure to choose his words carefully, "We all have things in our life that are hard to share or come to terms with. From what I know about your dad, I'm sure he was trying not to hurt anybody until he could figure things out."

"A year and a half though James."

James took a moment for a quiet reflection.

"I'm not here to judge him, I can't speak for how he handled the situation. I'm sure he's glad now that it's all out in the open. Right now, I'm only concerned about how you are doing."

"I'm fine but I think I'd like a glass of water if you don't mind."

"Glass of water coming right up."

Scarlett thought about James' remarks about her father, she knew he was right and she had seen first-hand how secrets could hurt people and confuse things.

Before she could talk herself out of it, she decided she would share a few secrets of her own.

James walked in with the glass of water.

"I need to tell you something and you need to be seated when I tell you."

Positioning his ears to hear, James said jokingly, "Alright, shoot. I'm all ears."

Scarlett started from the beginning.

"As you know, my mother is a consultant, she consults with churches on how they can become better. Well, growing up I used to attend a lot of churches with her as she was building her consulting practice. At every church, whether big or small, I noticed how well the pastor's wives were treated. You know, I've had time to think about this and figure this out and you are actually the first person I'm admitting this to."

James settled into his seat with a focused mind, listening intently, "Okay, I'm listening."

"I think growing up, I believed I could become a first lady, I felt like all that I'd seen, I could have done it with ease. I couldn't understand why but there was something about that role that appealed to me."

Scarlett drank a sip of water. Her mouth was already drying up and she hadn't even gotten to the good parts.

"Many years ago, I accompanied my mother on a church trip out to California, a huge church with a well-known family in ministry, the Montgomery family."

"I think I may have heard something about them before."

"Yeah, I wouldn't be surprised, they are very well known. Anyway, during her visits there, I met and fell in love with their oldest son, Carson. He swept me off my feet and sold me on this promise of a beautiful life together. His promises and my hidden desires collided. We married and I became a first lady."

"A first lady, huh?"

"Yeah, what a joke right?

Scarlett's voice began to quiver, the pain of her past was still present.

"Almost a year ago, I discovered my husband was cheating on me with a woman named Rebekkah. I never questioned him about it because even though I hate to admit it, I didn't want to confront him. Confronting him would only disrupt my cushy life."

Admitting the truth was hard but Scarlett found strength to continue on.

"I came home one day and my husband proceeds to tell me I'm not the woman he thought could help him lead the church and that he's found someone who can. He lays out my life for the next five years. He concocts a story about how the life of a first lady is not for me and I can't handle it and as a result, I up and leave him. When all the while, he's set it up for me to essentially fall off the face of the earth in exchange for spousal support for the next five years."

"Is that even legal?"

"According to our prenuptial agreement, he felt like he was justified. Carson behaved like a lonesome man in a lawless land. He made me an outlaw to a family I loved dearly, leaving me to face a whole new frontier all alone. Or so I thought."

"You're working those western references tonight aren't you?"

"James, don't pick at me."

"I'm only trying to lighten the mood a little."

"I thought I'd come and hang out with my parents for about a week, regroup, and figure out where I was heading next. During that week, I found out I was pregnant. I'm divorced and pregnant all in the same week. But you know what, this baby has been my case for survival."

She'd placed her own self in the hot seat and needed to get up and stretch.

"So, this is the long and short of who I am. Can you see why now I can't be seen as the mastermind behind my program? Because of Carson, I had to come up with a whole new way of life, another persona. He doesn't know I'm pregnant and I don't want him to know either. Oh yeah by the way, my name isn't Marilene."

"If your name isn't Marilene, what is your name?"

"Scarlett."

James stood up and extended his hand for a handshake, "Hello Scarlett, my name is James and it's very nice to meet you."

Scarlett slapped James across his chest, "James, don't be silly, I'm serious here."

Scarlett thought for a moment.

"Hey, wait a minute. Why don't you seem surprised by what I've told you?"

James now had to make a confession of his own.

"Scarlett, I'm going to have to get used to calling you that. Do you mind if I call you Red?"

"You must want me to slap you."

"Only if you promise to slap me and never let me go."

"James, answer me. Why is it you seem unmoved by what I've said?"

"Because I knew or let me say, I had an idea. The thing is none of it matters to me. I could care less who you were married to before."

"What do you mean you had an idea?"

"Jesus woman, if you must know, the day you met Alicia, she felt like she'd seen you before. She let her suspicions get the best of her and she found some old church programs her mother had. Apparently, her mother attends that church and she confronted me about you."

"Alicia, huh?"

James turned Scarlett towards him, holding onto her shoulders, "Listen to me, none of this matters to me. Your past isn't as important to me as your future. When I saw the pictures, I wasn't sure if it was you and neither was she. I decided that night you must've had a reason for not sharing that part of your life with me. I said to myself if and when you were ready, I'd be here to support you."

Telling James the truth was liberating, she didn't know how to connect the emotion she was feeling from opening up to him. She felt vulnerable but it wasn't a bad vulnerability it was an empowering one.

Holding James in an embrace, she took a chance, "If you're here to support me, show me by kissing me right now."

James had envisioned this moment for weeks now but never thought she'd be leading the charge. Albeit unexpected, the moment could not have been more right.

The loving vibe pulsating between them bubbling up into a deep and lingering kiss they both yielded to.

For a moment, the two thought they were hearing bells as they kissed but it was the constant ringing of the doorbell that interfered with their first romantic encounter.

CHAPTER 48

"**O**h Dr. Hartgrove, please help us. Please help, we've already called 911 but they are taking too long. We ran over here to see if you would help us...please."

James' next door neighbors, the Alexander family was frantic at his front door step. Michelle Alexander moaned in anguish as her husband, Drew spoke with an emotion-choked voice.

"Dr. Hartgrove, we decided to grill out tonight and eat by our pool. Michelle and I were clearing the table from dinner and we turned our backs for a second."

Holding the tiny, lifeless body that belong to two-year-old Sasha, Drew continued on, "We thought Sasha was following us as she normally follows Michelle foot-to-foot."

Michelle rocked in place at the door, on the edge of losing her mind completely.

"When we walked back outside we saw our precious little baby floating in the water."

James didn't wait to hear the rest of the story, he grabbed the toddler and immediately began to administer CPR, trying to resuscitate the child.

Scarlett said a quick prayer and tried to comfort the parents while James went to work until the paramedics arrived.

Michelle pounded her fists up against the walls in the foyer, "I was only gone for a second. Lord, please don't let my baby die. Please God, I'll do anything."

Scarlett winced at Michelle's pain, she shuddered to think of what she must be going through in that moment.

Twice now Scarlett had witnessed James without question jump into action to help save someone. Seeing him tonight, utilizing his hands for healing deepened her feelings for him.

Living through the terrifying episode, it seemed as if time stood still, however, time started again when little Sasha chocked up and gurgled on the residual pool water.

Scarlett heard the sirens and saw the lights from inside of James' home, she went outside to direct the paramedics over to where the family was.

Drew looked at James, man to man, "There is no way I can ever repay you. Thank you for helping to save my little girl's life. I owe you."

James got choked up, "You don't owe me anything. Go, go on a head to the hospital and I'll check on you all later."

James had saved the day once again and Scarlett was thrilled to be a part of it.

Plopping down on the sofa, James exclaimed, "Today has been a day. How are you holding up over there?"

"I'm fine, I think seeing what just happened made me realize how fragile life is. We should never take it for granted. It can be taken from you in the blink of an eye."

"Yeah, you're right. I know about that all too well. It's getting late, do you think you want to go back home or are you going to hang out over here with me?"

Scarlett felt like there was a story behind his words. She snuggled next to him laying her head on his chest, "Do you want me to stay over here with you?"

James lifted her chin up with his forefinger and kissed her softly and said, "What do you think?"

In an effort to see if there was a story, she did a little digging, "I know you are a doctor and all but seeing you now with baby Sasha and Liam the other day, you seem to be driven by something other than just being a doctor. Is that the case or am I imagining things?"

Having a draining day would not stop him from opening up, she'd been transparent with him and it was now time for him to be open with her.

"Very long story short, I lost my girlfriend to congenital heart failure and I couldn't do anything about it. The great Dr. James Hartgrove couldn't do anything to save her. I failed her. From the moment she died, within my power, I knew I wouldn't be able to live allowing another person slip through my fingers."

"James, I'm so sorry."

"No need to apologize. I have accepted everything happens for a reason but I'm going to do whatever I can to help people. Now you see why the health expo is so important to me. She helped me start it but I do it now in her honor."

Scarlett held his hand up and kissed it, "I'm glad to be a part of the health fair and I pray it works out well. I'm not saying this because I'm involved but I believe this year is going to be the best year ever."

CHAPTER 49

"Godfrey, this is Rebekkah, do you mind meeting us at the hospital, I'm on my way to the emergency room with Carson."

"Alright, okay. I'll be there as soon as possible. I'll leave right now."

Rebekkah drug Carson inside of the hospital's emergency room. He wouldn't go to the doctor on his own. At best, things had been strained between the two since the baby shower ordeal. Nevertheless, she was no longer willing to sit around and watch his pride cause him to self-destruct.

"So, what brings you in here tonight folks? What sort of symptoms are you having?"

Carson wouldn't answer.

Rebekkah spoke up.

"I think he's losing weight."

"He's having recurring nose bleeds."

"The reason I brought him in tonight was because in his sleep, he was choking with shortness of breath and he completely soaked our sheets from sweat."

The doctor looked Carson over, "Sounds like a case of the flu, there is a bad strain going around but let's see here."

As the doctor was examining him, Godfrey showed up.

Godfrey Carmicheal was Carson's head armor bearer. Godfrey had been recently named the official trainer for the armor bearer ministry at Wondrous Works.

Even though the administration of the New Testament church makes no reference to the position, Godfrey believed he was serving faithfully in a role he'd been called to serve in. His only gripe, he'd been assigned to Carson for too long. Carson treated him like his very own personal concierge.

Carson was chilled to the bone. Through chattering teeth, he said, "What's he doing here?"

"Carson. I called Godfrey. Aside from your family, he's the closest person to you."

Godfrey hadn't really paid attention to Carson's health. Carson had been putting his best foot forward, trying to ignore the signs his body was screaming at him.

For the first time, seeing him lying up in the hospital bed, he saw Carson in a different light with his unkempt appearance and paper-thin skin.

"Rebekkah, do you mind if I speak to you for a moment?"

Godfrey and Rebekkah walked outside of the examination room, standing away enough from Carson's earshot.

"Wow, he doesn't look so well. What's going on? Have the doctors said anything yet?"

"They are running a few tests but the doctor seems to think it's a really bad case of the flu. I hope that's all it is. He's been so...I don't even know how to describe it."

Godfrey touched Rebekkah in the small of her back, "You don't have to tell me. That Carson is something else. What I want to know is, how are you holding up?"

Rebekkah folded her arms across her chest, "I guess I'm doing alright. We've been really going through lately and I just never bargained for any of this. He's been so distant and I'm trying to do all I can but nothing is working."

Touching her again, Godfrey comforted her, "Hey listen, you don't deserve to be treated any kind of way. I have seen the way Carson treats women and you'd think after what happened with his first wife, he would have learned his lesson. He's lucky to have a woman like you by his side."

Rebekkah was grateful to Godfrey, she was appreciative of his encouraging words. She needed his shoulder to cry on. His words of comfort seeped into the crevices of her heart that were now tattered from her husband.

"The doctor is coming back, let's see what the results are."

Godfrey and Rebekkah walked back in to see Carson fast asleep. Even in his sleep he seemed tormented.

The doctor declared his confirmation, "Just as I suspected, Mr. Montgomery, you have the flu. I'm going to prescribe you a round of aggressive antibiotics and you should be feeling better in about a day or two."

Rebekkah expressed her gratitude, "Thank you doctor. I'm glad it's just the flu. We'll get him started on those meds as quickly as I can get them filled. Our pharmacy is closed this time of night. Is it possible to get the prescription filled here?"

"I hadn't thought of that, I've been working around the clock, I wasn't aware of the time. Wait here, I'll get it filled for you."

"Rebekkah, I'll help you get him in the car. Do you need for me to come over?"

Rebekkah always enjoyed Godfrey's company, it might be nice to have someone to help her with Carson.

"Yeah, I think that might be a good idea. But, first can you call his parents and let them know what's going on and that we won't be at church tomorrow?"

"Give me your keys, I'll go and pull your car around and I'll call them while I do that."

Rebekkah looked at Godfrey and smiled, "Thanks Godfrey."

Back at Carson and Rebekkah's home, Godfrey assisted Rebekkah with getting Carson his medicine and into bed.

That night Godfrey and Rebekkah stayed up talking, laughing, and having a great time.

Spending time with Godfrey was a welcomed distraction from all of the drama she and Carson had been recently going through.

At the Montgomery home, the sun rising above the horizon signaled the dawn of a new day.

CHAPTER 50

"**B**lessed be the name of the Lord. Blessed be the name. Good morning Father, good morning Jesus, good morning Holy Spirit."

With her hands raised, Regina woke up every morning with that saying.

"Good morning honey, did you sleep alright?"

Bishop rose up and sat on the edge of the bed, "I slept alright...and you?"

"I had a hard time sleeping after receiving that call from Godfrey. I'm worried about Carson honey. I can tell something isn't right with him."

"Now Regina, you can't go over there trying to fix it or fix him. He has a wife, let her do her job."

In a huff, Regina threw the covers off, "Her job huh, I've seen the kind of work she does. All she did was run his real wife off."

"Regina."

"It's true and you know it."

Bishop still seated on the edge of the bed never turned to look at his wife, his back was turned to her the entire time.

Regina lying in bed with her hands above her head, "Sometimes I wonder, where did we go wrong with Carson? Do you think we put too much pressure on him growing up? In all actuality, we did, to some degree overindulge all three of them. It can be hard raising children while working in the ministry, with so many demands on your time."

Regina rambled on more and more.

"I really don't know what to think anymore. What I do know is that I'm concerned."

"I am too but I can't do anything about any of it. All I can do is give it to the Lord and let Him work out the rest. Carson hasn't been to service in weeks, he should've been speaking, and preparing to assume the role and now he's sick. Interestingly enough, Christian called me last night and said he'd step in and speak today. I told him I'd think about it and let him know."

Regina sat up, "What did you decide?"

"I called him back and told him yes."

Regina scratched her neck, "So are you thinking of letting Christian take over?"

"Regina, I'm not thinking anything but I'm prayerful about everything. Now may not be time for me to retire. I'm going to take one day at a time and see what happens."

CHAPTER 51

"**M**inta, please open the door. You aren't going to be able to stay in that room forever. At some point, you're going to have to face me. Come out now so we can talk...I made breakfast."

George stood outside of their guest bedroom door hoping to talk his wife up out of the room.

No response.

Touching the door one last time, wishing he was touching Minta, George staggered his way down the stairs into the kitchen.

After everyone stormed out the night before, Cole and Marissa decided to return back to school. Their news would have to wait. There was already too much going on and Scarlett had spent the night over at James' place.

The piping, hot coffee gave him a jolt as he drifted off rehearsing what he'd say to Minta if and when he ever saw her again.

Nothing seemed to sound right.

What could he say that would make the situation better?

He hadn't a clue but he was soon to find out if any of it would work.

Minta strolled down the stairs with a suitcase in tow. George noticed it.

"I didn't know you were planning to go somewhere?"

Minta poured a cup of coffee. The hot cup of caffeine wasn't enough to warm her chilled demeanor.

"And it's obvious, there's plenty I didn't know about you."

"Minta...really? Is that how you want to play this?"

Minta rolled her eyes, "You are sadly mistaken, this is not a game to me; I'm not playing anything."

George tried to get close to Minta.

"Sweetheart, will you please listen to me for a moment?"

Minta shot past him, increasing the distance between them.

"Listen to me please. I want to apologize to you and let you know how sorry I am."

"What are you sorry for George because I don't think you really get it? Are you sorry for ruining a beautiful end to a wonderful time of celebration for our daughter? Are you sorry for allowing that little twerp to come into our home and disrespect me the way he did? I see his mama didn't teach him any manners. But better yet, are you sorry for not even telling me about the little pip-squeak in the first place?"

"All of the above and you don't have to call him names. He hasn't done anything to you."

Minta took in a huge breath, "Oh really now, he hasn't done anything to me. According to you, we are here in the God forsaken country town because of him. We were supposed to be spending our golden years together living the high life not establishing relationships with long lost children. You never even mentioned a Nadine Raulerson to me, I thought I knew about all of your past girlfriends. I questioned you and questioned you about why here and you could have been honest and told me the truth then but you decided to lie to me over and over again."

"Minta, she was never my girlfriend and right now, you're acting like I cheated on you with her."

"You may not have cheated on me but you've certainly cheated me out of what we've worked so hard to create."

"We still can have everything we wanted. But look, can't you see that moving here was the best thing? I believe it's you always saying, all things work together for good. As soon as we moved here, our daughter needed us. Carson would have never thought we'd be here let alone Scarlett. He wanted her to disappear and by her coming to us, we essentially had to do the same thing. You even sold your business so he wouldn't be able to track us down, so all I'm saying is that there is some purpose in it."

The verbal sparring between George and Minta was steady. She was intent on deliberately jabbing him with inflammatory remarks. Minta was suffering from an inability to relate to George in a rational manner.

"Minta, outside of telling you from the very beginning, which I've admitted was wrong, please tell me when the timing was right for me to tell you. Trust me honey, I wanted to tell you. I was torn. Travis grew up without a father and I felt guilty. I felt like I owed him an opportunity to get to know and have a relationship with me. There, I said it...I was guilty. He didn't grow up like Cole and Scarlett honey, his life was tough."

Minta tossed her mug into the sink, "Well you can have all the relationship you want with him but it will be without me. I've decided to take a last minute consulting assignment; I'm getting ready to fly out so I can make it to their first service. I will be extending my stay there for the week. Scarlett has the expo coming up and I'll be back in time to attend that with her."

George begged Minta for her forgiveness, his shoulders quaked with repressed sobbing. He had never seen her like this before.

"Minta, we've been through too much to let this destroy us. Tell me what I can do to make this right between us. Now, I refuse to believe that my wife, the one who preaches forgiveness and provides encouragement to others is choosing to hold grudges. I love you honey."

Minta grabbed her bag and walked into the garage, "Good-bye George; I'll be in touch."

CHAPTER 52

"I can't believe today has finally arrived. Prayerfully, all of our planning and hard work will pay off in a big way today."

The excitement was through the roof at James' office as he and Alicia were packing up some last minute items before heading to the venue.

Scarlett was on her way to James' office with hopes of surprising him with an impromptu breakfast. She wanted to spend a little alone time with him before all of the festivities began.

"Oh wow, I'm so excited. I can barely contain myself. Walking and talking is about to be launched from an official platform in front of thousands. Lord, if You would have told me I'd be here a year ago, that this would be my life I would have laughed You out of town. Oh but I'm so glad to be at this place in my life. Thank You for all of Your many blessings."

Scarlett pulled up and parked in between James' SUV and Alicia's convertible sports car.

"Alicia's here, great."

Scarlett gathered up her breakfast goodies and proceeded to enter the office. She knew where the spare key was kept.

"Are we all packed up and ready to go Alicia?"

Alicia's eyes were fixated on James, they smoldered with intensity; she followed his every move. She'd been paying him compliments all morning, grasping at any attempt to make their conversations be about the two of them working together. There was something about the anticipation of the expo that made her decide to throw caution to the wind and pounce.

"Before we leave there's one last thing that needs to be done."

"We've already spent too much time over here, I'm ready to go Alicia. Can whatever need to be done be done over at the place?"

Alicia suspected James might have a thing for who she now called the mystery woman but she felt like he's known her longer and they shared more of a history than the two of them. Not only that, she'd done so much work for him over the years, he should have been able to see her value and her worth.

Alicia moved in and angled her body towards James. She put his hands around her waist, grabbed his face between her delicate hands and said, "No, this can't be done over there, this is long overdue."

She planted her lips on top of his.

Straight away, James pushed her back, wiping his lips, asking, "Girl, what is wrong with you? Have you lost your mind? Are you seriously going to pull this on me today? I know it's time for me to get up out of here."

Alicia didn't say a word, she disconnected totally, wishing to escape by any means necessary.

James grabbed the remaining boxes and bolted out of his office, leaving Alicia behind.

Unbeknownst to him, Scarlett had just left them both behind. She left out and pulled around the nearest convenience store.

"I knew he was too good to be true."

Scarlett beat the steering wheel of her car like it was the one who had offended her.

"The moment I let my guard down and begin to trust I find out yet again that I'm not good enough for a man."

Scarlett sat in the parking lot trying to make sense of her scattered thoughts, she felt nauseated, her skin started to tighten.

Reaching for her phone to call Minta, she received a text message:

"GM Sunshine, 2day is the big day...I can't w8 2 c u!"

In haste, Scarlett threw the phone in the back seat, *"I just bet you can't wait to see me. Well you'll be waiting forever because you won't be seeing me ever again."*

The phone rang.

It was Minta.

"Hey, you left out early so I'm checking to see am I meeting you at the location, are we riding together, you coming back home, or what?"

"I'm coming home."

"Okay, I guess we're riding together then."

"Nope, I'm coming home but I'm not going."

"What do you mean you're not going? A lot has been put into this and now you aren't going? What happened? Where are you?"

Scarlett explained to Minta what transpired.

"Girl, James don't want no Alicia. You can always tell a man's object of affection because he shows it with his eyes. The woman who has captured his heart shines through his eyes and I don't see that nowhere near him when he looks at her."

"Mama, please...I'm not in the mood for one of your lectures right now."

"You may not be in the mood for a lecture so I'll keep it short. Now, I don't see that look with James and Alicia but I see it when he looks at you."

Minta grabbed her keys and her purse.

Scarlett tried to deflect, "Daddy looks at you like that."

"I'm not talking about me and your daddy right now. You need to stay where you are. I'm going to come and pick you up, we can kill some time and get some breakfast before we head over there."

Minta wanted to keep Scarlett on the line until she could get to her and see her face to face.

"Now Scarlett, are you seriously trying to tell me out of all you've been through, you're going to let this little misunderstanding stop you from enjoying the fruits of your labor?"

"Mama, you don't know it was a misunderstanding."

Minta smirked, "If I were a betting woman, I'd put all of my money on James. Look here, I'm going to need you to calm your little self, down. I don't need you getting upset and bringing my grandson here before he's ready."

Scarlett listened to the voice of reason, Minta was right. She wouldn't miss it; she wasn't particularly thrilled about going but at least she was now attending again.

CHAPTER 53

"It's been a week and Carson seems to be getting sicker, not better."

Godfrey called to check on Carson and Rebekkah, he'd been a tremendous source of support to the two of them.

"So you think he's not responding to the antibiotics?"

"No, not at all. The doctor said he would be feeling better in a few days and he's still sick."

Carson was getting more and more sick and Rebekkah was getting more and more sick of him. The life he'd promised her was evaporating.

"How did he handle hearing that Christian was the speaker at church last week?"

Rebekkah lowered her head and then popped it back up, "I think the thought of Christian or anyone other than him taking over Wondrous Works is killing him more than whatever else is going on with him."

Rebekkah and Godfrey both laughed. Deep down, they both knew Carson did not want to be dethroned. The problem was, his master plan was being ripped apart at the seams.

"Godfrey, do you know by chance who's speaking tomorrow?"

"I'm here at the church now, I was here for an early morning meeting and from what I understand, Christian is speaking again tomorrow."

Rebekkah ran her fingers through her hair, "This is not good. I'm going to take Carson back to the hospital. Somebody is going to tell us something today. I'm not leaving until I know what's going on. We need to figure out what is wrong with him so he can get better."

"I think you're right. Let me finish up here at the church and I'll come over and drive you all to the hospital. You shouldn't have to deal with this by yourself. I'll let his family know and I'll be there soon."

Rebekkah's lips trembled, "Thanks Godfrey, you've been a true Godsend, having you here supporting us means the world to me. I'll see you in a little bit."

CHAPTER 54

"Scarlett, girl...everything here looks amazing. Your program is being featured on the center stage. Will you look at God?"

Scarlett was hesitant but she did for a minute allow herself to feel the reward of the moment. As her mother had predicted, this was truly the Lord's doing and it was marvelous.

"Are you going to let James know that we are here?"

"Don't push it woman, I'm not ready to see him. Let me do this how I need to do it. Right now, I'd like to walk around and take in the event."

The exhibition center was filled with thousands of attendees. From wall-to-wall vendors, prizes, samples, the kid's play area, and the live demonstrations, there was something there for everyone.

A local news personality walked the crowd scouting for people to interview, the reporter and camera man happened to stop in front of Minta and Scarlett.

"Do you mind if we interview you for our news segment that'll be featured on the news tonight?"

"Uh, no thanks. We'll pass."

Minta and Scarlett politely by passed the two looking confused.

The reporter turned to his sidekick, "That's weird, who doesn't like being interviewed for the news?"

The mother and daughter team made their way around the entire showroom floor looking, admiring, and sometimes buying from all of the vendors.

On their route they ran into Carlos who was offering free massages and minor adjustments from his chiropractic clinic.

Minta stopped for a massage.

"Scarlett, do you think you might want to get adjusted?" Carlos offered.

Scarlett was about to take a seat, "Oh yes, I'm sure I could use it. This baby is wearing me out today."

Minta put a screeching halt to that plan with the quickness, waving her hands in the air, "Oh no, there will be no adjustments done on her, she's pregnant. We're not taking any chances with the baby."

Carlos smiled, "With all due respect ma'am, chiropractic care should be a part of every pregnant woman's regime. The adjustments help alleviate some of the stress and pressures placed on the body during pregnancy. In most cases, it can boost the chances of an easier delivery."

Minta started talking about all the things that could potentially go wrong.

Scarlett stood up and said, "Thanks Carlos. I'll remove the crazy woman from your booth. Good luck today with everything."

Scarlett's swayed back trot slowed down a bit, she lingered around to catch her breath. At this point in her pregnancy, she was experiencing shortness of breath more frequently.

"Are you okay? Do you want to sit down and take a break?"

Scarlett joked around, "I'm alright mama. I do think my little man is protesting though. I think he wanted his mama to get her free adjustment."

A spokesperson for the local cord blood bank stopped Scarlett and Minta before they started walking again.

"Excuse me. I couldn't help but see you'll be expecting a little one very soon. May I ask if you've ever heard about banking your baby's cord blood?"

The representative handed both ladies brochures.

Scarlett acknowledged, "I've never even heard of such. What is it?"

"Essentially, the blood from your umbilical cord is powerful, it can in some cases save people's lives. It contains precious stems cells that could be used in transfusions for people who are suffering from a number of diseases. By banking the blood, it's like having an insurance policy, when you don't have it, you wished you did and when you do, you're grateful it's there."

Scarlett handed the brochure back, "Sounds like a gimmick to me."

Being the aggressive sales lady she was, "No, not at all. There are documented studies coming out every day how cord blood banks, private and otherwise are using this blood to save lives. I think it's definitely worth taking a look at. We are only here trying to spread the word and especially with women who are pregnant because this can only be retrieved at birth."

Minta was intrigued, she began to ask more elicit questions to glean more information.

The representative shared more facts and finding with them.

"Honey, you never know what might happen. I think you should consider it. It's like organ donation. If you look at my driver's license, you'll see I'm a certified organ donor. Hey, if something happens to me, I pray something I have can help somebody else. Who knows my little grandson might be able to do the same."

Scarlett knew how important organ donation was to her mother. When Minta was a young girl, her mother died waiting on a kidney transplant.

Scarlett gave a partial concession, "Alright, alright. I'll pray about it and see what happens. It might be nice to know that my baby helped someone. We'll see."

Minta and Scarlett continued to scout out the vendors while also relishing in the purview of the center stage.

"Oh wow, what do we have here?"

Minta and Scarlett walked up on a booth featuring local celebrities hosting a live essential oils demonstration.

The hosts were using all of the right words to get the crowd engaged, therapeutic, medicinal, healing, healthy, builds immunity, the way nature intended, these statements resonated with the mindful supporters.

"I believe everything they are saying honey, I've had very little experience with oils but I've always wanted to know more about them."

"Then you should go up there and get more information mama, go see what's up."

Minta made her way to the front of the line. She was fascinated by everything she heard. After about a half an hour, Minta came out with several bags and a new vocation, she had signed up to become a distributor of the essential oils.

Scarlett saw her mother and couldn't help but laugh, "Mama, I see they got you good. You just couldn't help yourself, huh?"

"Oh nah honey, I've been trying to think about what I was going to do after I finished these last consultations. There is no way I'm getting ready to be stuck up under your daddy every day all day. This is getting ready to be my little side gig, I can do this and still spoil my little grandbaby. I'm excited now, c'mon let's see what else is out here."

James had not been able to reach Scarlett at all that morning. Despite being pulled into one million different directions; he was beginning to worry. He decided to take a small break.

Scarlett and Minta had been at it for a while and Scarlett now felt the need to sit down and rest for a minute. They decided to go to the food area and grab a snack.

As Minta and Scarlett made it to the concession stands, Scarlett heard someone call for her, in a name no one there should have known. The hair on the nape of her neck lifted.

The calling wouldn't stop, "First lady Scarlett, hello...is that you? First lady, it's me Priscilla."

Priscilla Hamilton was ducking through the crowd in a relentless pursuit trying to get Scarlett's attention.

Scarlett's eyes began to blink rapidly, looking all around trying to locate the voice calling out to her. She froze, she couldn't move or say anything; she felt like her feet had planted roots beneath her.

"Honey...Scarlett baby, talk to me. What's going on with you? Do you need to sit down, what's wrong?"

Minta's questions became frantic. As she tried to move Scarlett towards a seat, Priscilla Hamilton walked up with her daughter, Alicia.

Priscilla hugged Scarlett and said, "It's a miracle, I thought I'd never see you again. I'm so glad my daughter invited me to come out here for this event or I would have never gotten to see you. She told me you might be here."

Alicia stood with a look that radiated superiority, she was supremely confident in herself. She'd been right the entire time and James would soon find out.

All at once, Scarlett trembled, her stomach tightened, it was rock solid, pain crossed her chest, and her bladder loosened.

Trying to hold Scarlett up long enough to get her seated didn't last and Minta buckled under Scarlett's pressure. Scarlett passed out in Minta's hands and they both fell to the floor.

Pure pandemonium broke out, mayhem ensued as Minta panicked searching for someone to help her daughter.

With all of the chaos, James ran to pinpoint the problem. Nothing could have prepared him for what he was about to see.

He broke through the crowds to find Alicia and her mother looking horrified and Minta losing it as the paramedics were hoisting Scarlett onto the stretcher.

Alicia turned out to be the landing pad for James' blown fuse, he went off, "What have you done? Did you have something to do with this? You better pray to God that nothing happens to her or her baby."

CHAPTER 55

"How long does it take for them to come back and give me a stronger antibiotic? All they need to do is give me something stronger to knock out this pesky little flu I have so I can get up out of here."

"Carson, we need to let the doctors do their jobs. I'm not leaving here until we know for certain what's going on with you."

"Rebekkah, you can't keep me here."

Godfrey spoke up, "But I sure can."

Even though he was weak, Carson figured he could get by Rebekkah but he knew full well he didn't want to try Godfrey.

Rebekkah needed a break, they'd been at the hospital for several hours, "It's lunchtime and I'm hungry. I'm going to go down to the cafeteria, do you guys want anything?"

Carson brushed her off.

Godfrey answered, "No thanks. Will you be okay?"

Rebekkah looked over at Godfrey and nodded, "Yes, I'll be fine. Thanks for asking though."

"Will she be okay, I'm the one sick here. Your loyalties should lie with me or have you forgotten that Godfrey?"

Godfrey stood up, he was not going to be affected by Carson's comments, "No, I haven't forgotten where my loyalties are but I think you have."

Carson scoffed, "And what is that supposed to mean?"

"Man, I've watched you go through so many women until it's not even funny. You're supposed to be a man of God, when you think you are a god. You not only had one great and beautiful wife but two and you just run over them like they are nothing."

Carson started to taunt Godfrey, "Oh does Godfrey want one of my wives? Is that what the problem is, are you jealous?"

Godfrey had no filter, "Look at you man. Why would I be jealous of you? You treat women like they are disposable and that you aren't. Women need a man who will care for their heart, when you do that for them, there isn't anything they won't do for you."

Carson tried to downplay what Godfrey was saying to him, "Yeah, like I'm going to listen to you."

"Whether you do or don't, I'll still say this, you can mess around if you want to but when you don't take care of home, home has a way of taking care of itself with someone else."

Shifting his body, Carson leaned in, "Sounds like you're speaking from personal experience playboy?"

Godfrey sat back down, "Take it for what you want...playboy."

The door opened, it was Rebekkah followed by two doctors.

"Sorry to keep you here so long folks but we wanted to run a battery of tests to make a determination as to what's going on."

The main doctor speaking continued on trying to get Carson, Rebekkah, and also Godfrey to trust him.

"You've been experiencing a lot of symptoms lately that appear and show up like the flu, right. Well, according to the labs we've done, your test results show that you have what is called, Acute Myelogenous Leukemia."

The doctor waited to let his diagnosis sink in.

Carson sat stone faced staring at the clock on the wall. It was twelve o'clock noon.

Rebekkah broke down and started crying.

Godfrey lowered his head.

The doctor asked, "Does anyone have any questions?"

Godfrey spoke up, "Can you please explain what his diagnosis really means?"

"Absolutely. Carson has what is called adult onset Leukemia, essentially, cancer of the blood."

Rebekkah asked, "Cancer? Does he have a tumor somewhere?"

"No ma'am, unlike other cancers, Leukemia doesn't have a tumor, the cancerous cells are typically found throughout the body."

Carson still hadn't spoken a word.

Godfrey inquired again, "What's next doctor? I mean, is there a way to treat this, or -?"

Carson yelled out, "Or what? It would suit you just right if I died, go ahead, that's what you were going to say isn't it?"

Rebekkah tried to censure Carson, "Don't do that Carson. Godfrey is only trying to help."

"There are various treatments and we can discuss which ones might be the best course of action for you. There's chemotherapy of course, there are other targeted therapies we've been having good success with, and we've also been seeing great progress with stem cell transplants."

The other doctor stepped in, "I know this isn't easy information to hear but we are going to do what we can to help you through this. There are patients who have beat this thing and those who go on to having a wonderful quality of life. We're going to start you on a round of medications now and we'd like to see you early next week to begin discussing your program of care."

The doctors finished up with their suggestions and recommendations and left the room.

Godfrey pulled Rebekkah aside, "What do you want me to do?"

"Can you go and get the car? I should probably call his parents huh, what do you think?"

Godfrey grabbed Rebekkah by the hand, offering his assurance and support, "I can call them while I get the car. I'll let them know what's going on."

Rebekkah squeezed his hand, "Thank you, I really appreciate you being here Godfrey."

Godfrey lifted Rebekkah's downturned chin, "Hey, listen...you don't have to go through this alone, I'm here for you."

CHAPTER 56

"George, I'm over here."

George ran over to find Minta waiting in the hallway. Scarlett had made it to the hospital and they were feverishly trying to stabilize her. Her blood pressure had dropped precipitously and it caused her body to go haywire. The stress had caused her water to break. She was unresponsive but the baby was on his way.

"I put a call into Cole, he said he and Marissa would get right on the road. They should be here in a few hours."

Minta tried to remain in faith, from the moment Scarlett passed out, she started praying but she was experiencing real human emotions. Things had been tense with George but she was grateful to have him there during this time.

Driving her fists into her legs, "Nothing can happen to them George, I want them to be alright."

George reached in and held her, he was trying to be strong but he was worried just the same.

Inside the room, Dr. James Hartgrove stood at the foot of her bed and watched as Scarlett was being hooked up to every type of monitor you could think of. Was this de-ja-vu all over again? Thoughts of Cheryl flashed through his mind, the day she died and here he was again. This time he was not going to let Scarlett go. Instead of using his hands, this time, he used his heart.

"Lord, this woman coming into my life has been exactly what I needed in order to start living again. I live to see her smile and to make her happy, I need her in my life, her and the baby. Father God, I'm asking You not to take them away from me. I promise You, Lord that I will spend my days loving and taking care of them until the day I die. I will cherish her just as You do for Your church. Lord, I love her, please bring her back to me. In Jesus's name, I pray. Amen."

The nurse exclaimed, "She's starting to wake up."

James rushed by her side, grabbing up her hand. He wanted to be the first person she saw when she opened her eyes. He used his other hand to slide his fingers through her hair.

Scarlett slowly opened her eyes.

"Hello there gorgeous, don't you ever scare me like that ever again."

Scarlett sat up in the bed, looking puzzled, "What am I doing here? How did I get here? Did I have the baby already? I'm confused. Wait a minute. James, what happened?"

James settled her down, he placed her hand over her stomach, "Look, see... you feel that? You're still pregnant and everything is going to be alright. However, your water did break and they've started to induce your labor."

"I just turned thirty-seven weeks today James, it's not time for him to come out. It's still early yet."

James could tell Scarlett was foggy on the details surrounding her reason for being admitted into the hospital and decided to not trouble her with them.

"Listen to me, you gave us a little scare earlier but you are in perfect hands. No one is going to let anything bad happen to you and this baby as long as I'm around."

As James continued to reassure Scarlett, he could not shake the feeling he'd felt after she'd awakened.

"Scarlett, I need to talk to you about something. I know it's going to sound crazy and I wouldn't blame you if you thought I was a crazy man but that's just it. I am crazy and I'm crazy about you. Having to think that I might lose you almost destroyed me. I don't ever want to experience being without you again."

Scarlett's eyes grew wide, "What are you talking about James?"

James bit the bullet, he went for it; "I guess what I'm trying to say is, marry me Scarlett. Will you be my wife? We can raise the baby together as our son."

Scarlett felt woozy, "James, this is too much. I...I, don't know what to say. What about -?"

"What about nothing, we'll figure everything out. Whatever it is, we'll cross that bridge when we get to it."

Scarlett sat up and repositioned herself in the bed, she didn't say anything for a long time. James waited for her to speak.

"I think you are an amazing man. I've been through a lot this past year and in some way, you've actually helped me to make it through. You know, I tried and tried all I could to push you away or keep you in a separate little box away from my feelings. Looking back, I guess it was all a form of protection, keeping you distant so you wouldn't have a chance to hurt me."

James declared to Scarlett, "I would never hurt you and the man who did is a coward but you don't have to worry about him anymore because I'm here. I love you Scarlett."

"That's what I'm trying to tell you. I'm not worrying about Carson, for all I care, he could drop dead in front of me and I'd walk right over him. Despite me trying to fight my feelings for you, I couldn't seem to break away from them. The type of person you are just drew me in like a magnet."

James started smiling, "If I'm such a magnet, let me draw you in a little closer."

Right as they were about to seal their agreement with a kiss, Minta barged in.

"Oh Lord, thank You Father, I praise Your Holy name. My daughter is awake."

Scarlett and James laughed in each other's arms.

"Mama, you are so dramatic. I'm fine and so is the baby."

James gave Minta an eye signal to indicate Scarlett's slight mental fogginess.

"Your father is out in the hallway, he wanted me to see what was going on in here before he came to see you. Are you sure you are alright honey?"

James made an offer, "If you don't mind, I'll go get George."

George was pacing the hallway, wearing out the sole of his new loafers.

"There he is, if it isn't George...George, the world famous."

George extended his hand towards James, "Hey how's my daughter doing? Is the baby alright?"

James smiled warmly, "Right now they are both doing fine."

George blew out a lot of reserved air, "What a relief. Thank you God for hearing our prayers."

"Yes, He has. Hey George, I have something I need to run by you real quick."

"What is it son?"

James was glowing, "Funny you called me son because I'd like to ask for your daughter's hand. I want to know if I have your blessing to marry your daughter."

George jumped for joy, "But of course you do. If you ask me, I would have preferred it had been you the first time around but hey, that's neither here nor there. With the baby coming, when do you think you'll get married?"

"Today."

"Whoa, today? You don't mess around do you boy?"

"Man, after what happened today, I'm not wasting any more time with that woman. I need her to know that I'm serious and committed to her and the baby. I'm changing both of their names today."

George placed his hand over James' shoulder, "You're a good man James. I do need to make you aware if you haven't forgotten that you can't consummate the marriage until after the baby is six weeks old."

James laughed at his soon to be father-in-law, "I do thank you for your concern but all of that will work itself out in its proper time and place. How I see it, Minta is a minister right, we can have a ceremony here in the hospital and then apply for our marriage licenses when Scarlett can get out of the house."

When Scarlett semi-accepted his proposal she didn't realize he meant get married that day.

"You want to get married here in the hospital? While I'm in labor? Have you lost your mind? Who does that?"

"A man in love that's who. I say why wait? I'm trying to prove to you how much you mean to me. I'm here with you for now and forever and we're getting ready to have a baby so you need to go ahead and say yes that you'll marry me."

It was settled. In a touching commitment ceremony, with Minta serving as the Officiate, George as the Best Man, and Cole and Marissa as the witnesses, Scarlett Watson and James Hartgrove pledged their love and committed their lives towards one another.

Hours later in a room filled with her brother, his girlfriend, her parents, and now her husband, Scarlett welcomed to the world, a bright-eyed, Chandler Eugene Watson Hartgrove weighing in at 6.5 pounds and 21 inches.

CHAPTER 57

"**J**ames, I need to run a few errands. Will you be okay with the baby while I'm gone?"

"Girl, what kind of question is that? Of course me and Chan the Man are going to be fine. You know this is how we roll. We are going to hang out here in the bed until you get back."

Scarlett kissed James, "You are so crazy but I love your crazy behind. Yes, I see how y'all roll. I'll only be gone for a little while."

Things had been going so well for the new family. After being released from the hospital, James brought home his new wife and son. Chandler was already four weeks old and thriving. After the expo, the blog had seen a spike in activity. The program was now being looked at for partnerships and joint ventures. Scarlett and James had applied for their marriage licenses, yet they still had the matter of consummation on the table.

Scarlett decided she didn't want to wait two more weeks. She was ready to physically express her love with James and tonight was going to be "the night." She was going to give the grandparents some time with their beloved Chandler so she could have some quality time with her beloved James.

She'd need to run out and shop for a few things to make the evening more special.

Scarlett grabbed her purse and opened the front door, "Well hello my dear. You opened before I could ring the doorbell. You look as beautiful as ever, I'm so happy to see you."

Scarlett's mouth flew open, she dropped her keys in the doorway. She stumbled over her words, "How did you know where to find me? What are you doing here? This is a gated community; how did you even get back here?"

"Scarlett honey, aren't you going to invite me in?"

Scarlett didn't extend an invitation, instead she walked out of the house and closed the door behind her.

"I'm not going to do anything until you answer some questions for me, Mama Montgomery."

"Alright dear, what do you want to know?"

Scarlett stood with her arms folded, "You can start by telling how you found me?"

"Do you remember a woman by the name of Priscilla Hamilton, she attends Wondrous Works and she sings in the choir?"

"No, what about her?"

The details surrounding Scarlett's preterm labor was still somewhat hazy to her and Minta and James didn't see the need to bother her with those details.

"Well apparently she was down here visiting her daughter and they attended an event where you were present. According to her, she tried to approach you and speak but you passed out. Then she said some man came out of nowhere and jumped all over her daughter, accusing her of doing something to you."

"Who is her daughter?"

"Her daughter's name is Alicia."

Scarlett cracked her neck from side to side, she didn't want to give her former mother-in-law any additional information. She wasn't sure of what she knew. Thinking to herself, *"Alicia better hope she don't ever see me in the street because if she does, she should be ready to get her tail tore up. Because of her, my baby's life was put in jeopardy, she better be glad he turned out alright. Now it makes sense to me why she's no longer managing the expo."*

"I'm sure you remember the luncheon you and I started, right Scarlett?"

"Of course I do, what about it?"

"Well, this year I spoke a totally different message and since then I've been getting all kinds of engagements to come and speak. Well, I've been out of town so much recently and Priscilla had been trying to meet with me. She stopped by my office and told me about seeing you. She was very concerned about you and what happened. Based on how she was I knew I needed to come and see you."

"But why?"

Regina reached in and grabbed Scarlett, "You have no idea how much I've been praying for you and hoping I'd get a chance to see you again."

"So, I guess Carson was telling the truth when he said you didn't know what he'd been planning."

Scarlett revealed to Regina the full scope of how Carson treated her and how he fabricated her disappearance. Regina could not believe her oldest son could even think of such a devious and wicked scheme. Nevertheless, she was still there for him.

"Priscilla came to tell me she'd run into you and how sorry she was for how everything happened. I asked her could she tell me where you were and she got all of the information from her daughter."

"Ole Alicia again, huh? Okay that explains how you found me but how did you get here and why are you here?"

"Christian and Courtney are getting married here next weekend and I'm here with them. I took a cab over here and then I paid a delivery man to bring me behind the security gate and here I am."

Scarlett couldn't help but laugh, "I see not much has changed with you. You are quite the resourceful one. But I still need to know why you're here?"

Regina rubbed her upper arms for comfort, "I need to tell you something. Now, based on what you said Carson did, you probably don't care but I still need you to hear me. Carson has been diagnosed with Leukemia."

Scarlett stood flat-footed in front of Regina and said, "So? And you are telling me this because?"

"Scarlett?"

"What? I'm seriously trying to find the moment where I begin to care? To be honest with you, a person couldn't even pay me to care about Carson."

Regina gasped, taking a step back. "My Lord Scarlett, this isn't like you."

"After all your son has done to me, why do you think it matters to me he's sick. He didn't care anything about me, he wanted me to basically fall off of the face of the earth. He didn't care whether I was dead or alive. He treated me like I was nothing. You know what, I hope you haven't told him anything about me."

"No, I haven't. I needed to see you first; I needed to make sure it was you. He needs a transfusion Scarlett. His doctors have prescribed several courses of actions but one they are hopeful on deals with stem cells."

Regina was fishing for information, testing the waters with Scarlett.

"Mama Montgomery, it's been nice seeing you and catching up but I was about to go somewhere when you showed up here at my house, unannounced. Can I take you somewhere or call you a cab?"

Regina could see she'd sparked a nerve within Scarlett and that Scarlett would love for nothing more than for her to leave.

"Is it true honey?"

"Is what true?"

"If what Priscilla told me is true, you had a baby. Is that baby, my grandbaby?"

Scarlett felt backed into a corner. It wouldn't be too long before the entire Montgomery clan would find out about Chandler. How could she handle this situation?

Regina got closer to Scarlett again, pleading to her, "None of us are potential matches for Carson and right now he needs a miracle. If what Priscilla said is true, there's a chance the baby could be a match."

Scarlett wouldn't confirm or deny Regina's contentions, "Like I said, it's been nice catching up, congratulations to Courtney and Christian, best of luck with Carson, and I'll be more than happy to give you a ride to the nearest cab stop."

"I know you're hurt and upset but before I leave, I appeal to you, if you are now a mother, you must know how a woman would go to the ends of the world to try and save her child. You think about that Scarlett. Mother to mother. I won't tell anyone I saw you, you have my word on that. Now take me up to the gate, I'll catch a cab up there."

CHAPTER 58

"Isn't Chandler just perfect? He's such a fine baby, I can't even seem to remember my life without him."

"Well you must have a short memory then Minta because that was only a month ago."

Minta picked up baby Chandler and snuggled him up, "I know it George. I could just eat him up. I wish I could protect him from everything bad in this world."

George didn't mince his words, "Everything bad like Carson, huh?" I told James, we'll all pack up and move again if we have to. I'm about sick and tired of the Montgomery's."

"Calm down George. Scarlett said Regina gave her word that she wouldn't say anything. Scarlett didn't let on about Chandler, Regina only had what that lady told her and that was it."

George tossed down his newspaper, "You think I trust them. They just get on my nerves Minta. Right when Scarlett starts to have some peace and happiness in her life, here they come again. They will not ruin her this time and certainly not the baby."

George reached for his grandson, "Hey there now buddy, Papa has you now. See how much he loves his Papa?"

"Yes I do but I think he loves his Mimi a tad bit more."

George and Minta could not have been more proud and happy to welcome their first grandson into their lives. Having Chandler around seemed to ease some of the tightness between them where Travis was concerned but it was still there nonetheless.

"Travis has called off and on to check on his sister and nephew."

Scoffing at George's announcement, "Good for him."

"Minta, will you give the poor guy a break? How long are you going to treat him like the proverbial, red-haired stepchild? Travis is a good guy. All he wants is to belong to a family. You can understand that, can't you? I mean, he didn't grow up like Scarlett and Cole, he and his mother had it hard. He didn't have the opportunities our kids had and I'm trying to make up some of that with him. You know, I think you'd actually like him if you got a chance to know him."

Minta grabbed Chandler back from George, "Look George, I'm trying but you've been dealing with this for far longer than me."

"Listen honey, I know it's going to take some time, for all of us, he and I are still getting to know one another but now that it's out in the open, I don't see why we can't all do it together?"

Minta performed a baby massage on Chandler and rubbed him down with some essential oils from her new venture. Chandler responded well to his grandmother's loving hands and rewarded her with a sound asleep baby boy.

Minta was enjoying learning about the health benefits of the essential oils, George teased her how she reminded him of his grandmother and how people used to call her an apothecary.

"You're really into these oils huh? Are you sure this isn't some hocus-pocus type stuff?"

"Now George you know I don't believe in anything hocus-pocus, now you didn't seem to have a problem the other night when you had your headache and I rubbed your temples with the peppermint oil from my kit. You told me the headache seemed to have melted away, did you not?"

George couldn't help but to laugh, "Yeah, I guess I did say that. Hmm, it really did work, just like that. I hate to change the subject but what about Travis, honey?"

Minta sat and rocked Chandler in the glider she'd purchased for their house, she bought it with the expressed intention on spoiling him in it.

"George, the best I can give you now is that I'm praying about it. No, Travis has not done anything to me but I feel like he has and you definitely did. Now I know I have to forgive but I'm working my way through it. Don't try and rush me, let me do it in my own way and in my own timing."

George got up and got Minta a glass of water, "I hear what you're saying honey. I promise I'll try and make this up to you; I never meant to hurt you. You're my wife and I love you. I'll try not to rush you."

"I appreciate you understanding where I'm coming from George. I'm kind of tired of talking about Travis right now if you don't mind. All I want to do is talk about this little guy right here."

George reached down and kissed them both on the cheek, "And that's fine by me."

CHAPTER 59

"I can't believe Carson and Rebekkah aren't going to be able to make the wedding." Bishop filled Courtney and Christian in on the severity of Carson's illness, "Yeah, my boy is in bad shape. His doctors have grounded him for the time being. With such a weakened immune system, they don't think it's in his best interest to travel."

"I can understand that but I'll tell you what, when I went to tell Rebekkah good-bye, she looks like she's in bad shape herself. She's been really going through with this situation."

Bishop Montgomery responded, "It's been tough on all of us, especially Regina but no matter what, we'll get through it...as a family. You know me, I choose to believe God."

The Montgomery entourage boarded the family jet and soared the airways to witness the nuptials of Christian and Courtney in a luxurious, Southern-styled wedding.

Rebekkah was left behind to care for Carson. Since his diagnosis, he'd gotten more difficult to deal with. Due largely in part to the fact he was having difficulty dealing with the mess of a life he'd made. He'd begun to retreat inward, withdrawing from everyone. He would never admit it aloud but in his quiet times, he'd often wish he could go back and change what he'd done.

Carson cried out to Rebekkah, she was now sleeping in another bedroom, "Hey Rebekkah, I need you for a minute."

"What do you want Carson?

"I need some water, I'm in a lot of pain and I want to take something for it."

"Alright, I'll be right back."

Her patience was growing shorter with him every day but she was prepared to stay and care for him over the weekend.

When Rebekkah returned with the tray of medicine, she thought she'd be nice and bring him something to snack on.

"Here you go Carson."

"I didn't ask you for that. All I asked you for was some water and for my medicine and you couldn't even do that right. Boy did I pick wrong when I picked you."

Carson swallowed his medicine, took a sip of water from the glass, and threw the rest onto Rebekkah.

She shrieked, that was it, she'd had it with him. Rebekkah left the room without saying anything else to Carson.

Several hours went by and the house grew dark and silent.

"Where is Rebekkah? It's time for my medicine and I'm ready to eat."

Carson called out to Rebekkah but this time there was no answer. He dialed her phone, there was not an answer there either.

Thirty minutes passed and Carson mustered up enough strength to check around the house for Rebekkah.

He made his way through the house and by the time he made it to the kitchen, he was winded but what he'd see next was sure to take more than his breath away.

Rebekkah was nowhere to be found but she had left Carson a note and it read:

Carson, in this past year, I have experienced some of the best of times and yet some of the worst of times. Unfortunately, the worst of times have started to outweigh the best of times. You promised me a lifetime of happiness and you lied. I didn't sign up for any of this stuff that has happened to us recently.

You are selfish, egotistical, hypocritical, and think this world owes you something. Well guess what it doesn't, but you will owe me. I figured I would decide to get out of this atrocity of a marriage before too much of my life was wasted on it. Since we never got that prenuptial agreement signed, you'll be hearing from lawyers soon.

I've arranged for some in-home care for you, where a nurse will come in and help you out until your parents come back from the wedding.

Good-bye and good riddance.

~ Rebekkah

Carson called Godfrey to see if he knew where Rebekkah was, Godfrey didn't answer either. It was not like Godfrey to not answer Carson's calls.

Carson staggered as he reread Rebekkah's letter. He was having trouble reaching anyone that night.

The pressure from the evening caused his knees to buckle under him, he'd finally hit the bottom of despair. He had nowhere to turn, his only option was to turn and look upwards toward heaven.

For the first time in years, Carson had a transformative experience where he cried aloud and spared not.

The next morning, the nurse found him on the kitchen floor, he'd been there all night.

CHAPTER 60

"Hey love, I know you asked me if I felt like I needed to go or wanted to go to California and I said no but I've been thinking and please don't be mad but I think I need to go."

James stretched and rubbed his eyes and ears, wanting to make sure he was completely engaged with his wife, "Okay, what changed your mind?"

Scarlett pulled her knees up to her chest, "I told you from the jump that I could care less about what was going on with Carson. On one hand, I could not believe his mother came all the way here to tell me about him and like I would want to help out and then on the other hand because she's a mom and that's her son, she's trying to do everything she can for him."

James perked up, "That's right and didn't you say she wasn't aware of what he'd done to you?"

"No, she didn't know. I was completely fine with going on like her visit didn't even happen but last night I had a horrible night. I tossed and turned and couldn't get back to sleep. I was kind of upset too because you and the baby were knocked out and I was up."

"I did notice a couple of times throughout the night you were quite restless. So, what are you thinking?"

Scarlett reached over to her night stand and showed James some papers.

"Since I couldn't sleep, I decided to get up and check my email, answer any blog comments if there were any, you know, the usual. I started checking and my inbox was filled with thank you letters from people that attended the health fair. The letters are talking about how they were motivated and encouraged by the simplicity of the program and how they've already begun to implement it and are already seeing changes. The letters that always seem to get me are the ones that say I have helped save their lives. Those are some big words to put on a person James."

"I guess you better get used to it."

"I haven't slept all night. The thing I struggle with is how can I have people saying things like this to me, that I'm helping them but when it comes to Carson, I have a mental block there. My mind has been racing all night, I've been trying to figure out what to do."

James embraced Scarlett, "He hurt you; from his hands you experienced a form of betrayal that rocked you to your very core. I don't know if you've actually had a chance to deal with that pain."

Scarlett sobbed in her husband's arms, he was right, because of the pregnancy she had not had a chance to really deal with the full ramifications of what happened to her.

Scarlett lifted her head and wiped her eyes, "I feel like I owe it to myself to go and face my accuser. Last year, I allowed him to dictate to me the conditions and what would happen with my life because I didn't think I had anything to fight him with. Oh but how things have changed."

"So when do you want to go?"

Scarlett hid slightly under the covers, "Um, like maybe today?"

James shook his head, "Girl, you never cease to amaze me. I take it you're trying to make it to their 11:00 o'clock service?"

"Yes, I'm thinking I just want to go, slip in and slip out, see what's up and leave."

James got up to make a phone call, "Let me call Dr. Rupert and see if he'll allow us to use his airplane, he's offered it to me so many times, I don't see why it should be a problem."

Scarlett got up and walked into her closet, "Babe, I think we need to probably dress a little incognito, what do you think? Let's do what we can to stay up under the radar, okay? As a matter of fact, I used to be close to the head usher there, he was like a grandfather to me. I wonder if he's still there, hopefully his number is still the same, I'm going to try him and see if he can get us in without being seen."

Everything had gone according to plan, Scarlett and James made it to the ornamental place of worship without incident. Scarlett was able to reach Bro. Oscar Robinson and she swore him to secrecy and he was more than happy to oblige her. James and Scarlett were tucked away upstairs in a room with one-way glass, you could see out but no one could see inside.

Scarlett sat next to James, biting her bottom lip, and rubbing her arms. James held her hand trying to quiet her nerves.

It was show time. The production of Sunday morning worship at Wondrous Works was starting. Service at Wondrous Works was something to behold, from the in-person encounter to the online streaming it was indeed an experience. Scarlett could see from the images dancing on James' eyeballs that he was taking in all of it.

"This is weird, I thought I would have been more nervous."

The program went on like clockwork, Scarlett pointed out to James people she remembered and missed. In a way, she felt like it was homecoming day at Wondrous Works.

The newlyweds were enjoying the service and the time was drawing nigh for the word of the Lord to be spoken, Bishop Montgomery would be speaking.

The praise team sang their sermonic song of praise before Bishop was to make his way to the podium.

Scarlett made herself comfortable to hear her former father-in-law speak. When the song was over, Bishop Montgomery began to walk across the stage but he stopped short of the sacred desk. Someone made it there before him.

It was none other than Carson Montgomery.

CHAPTER 61

"**S**orry Bishop but there's something I need to do and I need to do it now."

Scarlett stared down at the figure of the man who used to be her husband. He looked different, he was now so frail and fragile looking, unlike the way she last saw him.

"He must be really sick."

"How are you holding up honey?"

"I'm fine James."

From time to time, Scarlett had joked around that if she ever saw Carson, he'd better pray she wasn't carrying her six-shooter pistol because there would be a serious showdown between the two of them. However, seeing him on the stage, she couldn't pinpoint what she was feeling.

Carson held onto the stand for support, he started speaking but then he stopped. He started again, "Good morning everyone. I know y'all are waiting to hear from Bishop but I have something I need to say."

He overheard some of the murmurs from the congregation giving him permission to carry on, he went with it.

"There is a scripture in the bible that says, confess your faults one to another and pray for each other so that you may be healed. I stand before you all today admitting that I have some sins that need to be confessed."

Bishop Montgomery was still standing by Carson, he whispered to his son, "Do you really want to do this?"

Carson answered, "I not only want to but I have to Bishop."

"I'm here to acknowledge my transgressions and the sin that is ever before me. As many of you know, last year, I went through a divorce and then remarried. What you don't know is that I'm a liar and a cheater. I have done a horrible thing. I made up a story. I told everyone that my wife left me; I set it up for people to believe she'd left because she couldn't handle the pressures of being in the ministry. The truth is, that woman loved me with everything she had in spite of all my flaws. Yet, I pushed her out, I treated her like yesterday's trash all so I could marry my mistress."

The incredulous stares, the yelps, and dropped open mouths almost caused Carson to stop but he continued.

Carson smirked, "Do y'all want to hear something funny? The lie I told on Scarlett actually turned out to be true with Rebekkah. Hear it straight from the horse's mouth, my wife, Rebekkah left me last night, she's gone."

The people attending Wondrous Works that day were spell bounded, Carson had their complete attention.

Scarlett sat up and grabbed James' arm, "Shut the front door; I can't believe..."

Carson continued, "I've been diagnosed with Leukemia and until last night, I had not been doing well with my prognosis. I'm sick y'all but I don't believe God is through with me yet. No matter what happens to me, I knew I couldn't go another day without coming clean about all the dirt I've done before this great assembly of believers. The word tells us again that the earnest prayers of a righteous person has great power and produces wonderful results. I need all the prayers I can get."

Carson stopped for a brief moment and motioned for the band to follow him, "Last night in my kitchen, I was all down and out with nowhere to turn but up."

Carson started singing words from the song, "<u>Love Lifted Me</u>".

Many were surprised to hear the smooth and soul-stirring chords coming from Carson because he'd sat on his gift of singing for years.

But not anymore.

Today, he sang with conviction and from a place of meaning that transferred to the audience. They favored him with waving hands, joining him singing the song, and pleas for more.

Bishop Montgomery turned on his microphone and pronounced over the people as Carson and the congregation sang, "According to 1 John 1:9; if we confess our sins, He is faithful and just to forgive us our sins and cleanse us from everything we've done wrong. Paul wrote to us in Ephesians that in whom we have redemption through His blood, the forgiveness of sins, according to the riches of His grace. Church, we all fall short of His glory, which means we all have something to confess but the beauty is that His blood redeems us and forgives our sins."

Before Bishop could finish, throngs of people began to make their way down to the altar where they fell on their faces and began to repent before the Lord. They connected with the love Carson was singing of and it compelled them to move toward repentance.

For those who could not make it down, they lined the aisles. For those who couldn't make the aisles, they bowed at their seats.

The presence of God swept over those who were willing to receive it and it wasn't just at Wondrous Works.

Cayden-James had been streaming the service as he usually did ever Sunday. This Sunday, he along with other inmates were on their faces praying.

Courtney and Christian were streaming while on their honeymoon, they were kneeling in their hotel suite.

George and Minta were watching from their family room with tears streaming from both of their faces and their hands raised. Chandler cooed in his cradle as they worshipped.

Up in the hideaway room, Scarlett was hysterical but she had to be quiet with it. From the moment Carson started talking, James held her close. They sat with tears in their eyes moved beyond words. Scarlett was beside herself, she happened to look up on the wall where she noticed the clock; it was twelve o'clock noon on the dot. In that moment she thought, *"This is it, I can't believe he just did that but justice has been served."*

EPILOGUE

"Wow, what a service, huh? James and I are in our hotel room right now and I don't know what to do with myself."

"What an amazing but interesting year this has been. In my wildest dreams I never thought my life would turn out like this. I have the world's most loving husband and quite possibly the cutest baby boy I've ever seen."

"Throughout all of this James has been right by my side and supported me without question. He's told me he'll support me come hell or high water."

"Carson doesn't even know there is a baby Chandler. In every way that it counts, James is Chandler's father, he signed his birth certificate and he's officially adopted him."

"Let's talk about that service again. Carson has vindicated me; it wasn't the showdown I'd imagined but it was epic nonetheless. He confessed in front of the entire Wondrous Works congregation. It was like the word in action where my righteousness did in fact shine like the morning and I received justice at high noon."

"During this time in my life, my trust in God has skyrocketed. Had I not gone through this experience, I would have never known to trust in Him the way I do today."

"However, now I'm left with wondering whether or not I should try to help save his life. When I look at my son, as much as I'd like to see James in him, Carson seems to automatically shine through. I don't know why but I did give Chandler Carson's middle name and I did give him a "C" name like the other Montgomery men. Can someone please tell me why I did that? It's only a matter of time before the Montgomery's find out about him though. I'm too exposed and Regina knows a little too much."

"My mind is all over the place right now. I'm not afraid to ask for some advice, if you were me, what would you do? (**#WWYD**) I look forward to hearing what you all have to say."

Reach out to Scarlett on Twitter at ShakiraBelieves:
#WWYD
#HighNoonJustice

Email: shakirabelieves@gmail.com your suggestions on what she should do. In addition, if she could exact revenge on Carson what do you think would be the best strategy. You can also email me with the subject, **Carson's Revenge** for the chance to be featured in an upcoming companion product.

Psalms 37:6
"He will act and will make your righteousness shine like the dawn, your justice like high noon. (CEB)"

ABOUT THE AUTHOR

Shakira R. Thompson, a natural born storyteller who submitted to her God-given talents and in doing so, God showed up and made her a **BELIEVER.** He's transformed her into an author, publisher, and entrepreneur.

She is the founder of **Believer's Choice Media**, an inspirational content company dedicated to encouraging believers to live the life they were created to live on earth and beyond. She's penned five, well-received inspirational fiction novels with a sixth on the way.

With a renewed sense of purpose, Shakira is not only writing and speaking, she's living...living her life according to Ephesians 2:10:

"For we are his workmanship, created in Christ Jesus unto good works, which God hath before ordained that we should walk in them." (KJV)

Shakira is a proud Alumni of Florida A&M University in Tallahassee, Florida where she holds a B.S in Business Administration as well as an M.B.A. with a concentration in Supply Chain Management.

Shakira has always delved in the world of real estate, but most recently made it official. She is a Realtor®, licensed in the State of Florida, where she's the listing agent for EquityPro. Naturally, she's expanding the Believer's Choice brand and is in the process of developing Believer's Choice Realty, LLC.

Living her life with purpose has pushed her into her latest venture, co-hosting *The Dee Lee Show,* where she has the opportunity to encourage BELIEVERS over the airwaves.

Although Shakira may wear many hats these days, the most important role to her, is that of wife and mother.

Born and raised in Fernandina Beach, Florida, she now resides in Orlando, Florida with her family.

A SNEAK PEEK
The Love Bug

"IT'S TIME," the smiling bachelor concluded. A new year, a new beginning. Taking gallant strides into "Boites a Bijoux," looking like he'd walked off the set of an "Ebony Man" magazine shoot, Lionel decided he was ready to propose. A year had almost gone by and to him; that was long enough to know Marsha was 'The One' to share his life with, to grow old together.

At Boites a Bijoux, French for jewelry boxes, you don't just go there to buy gifts, you go there for the experience, their brand had been established by not offering jewelry but emotional experiences. From the moment you walk into the strategically designed showroom with brilliantly shining lights from above and dazzling glass cases sparkling yet protecting, you are not a customer but a member of the family who wish to help you celebrate life through jewelry. So when the melodic chimes rang throughout the store alerting Lionel's arrival, an associate from the Boites a Bijoux family was waiting for him.

"Welcome to Boites a Bijoux! Extending her hand for a warm handshake, the associate introduced herself, "I'm Maria Carne and I'm going to be your celebration specialist for the day. How may I be of service to you?"

Clearing his throat and smiling at the same time, "Nice to meet you Maria, I'm Lionel Webber and I'm here to pick out an engagement ring for my girlfriend."

Motioning for Lionel to follow her to an interview room, with a wide grin and eyes gleaming with excitement, Maria exchanged Lionel's introduction with a resolution, "I knew you had a reason to celebrate when you walked through those doors, you look like a man on a mission and I'm going to help you pick out a ring befitting your lady love."

Each person entering the store is escorted into an interview room for an initial consultation before going out onto the showroom floor. This way, the associates begin establishing long-lasting relationships with their customers by gathering a true understanding for the purpose of the gifts.

Maria shifted her casual conversation into more pointed questions, "So, what's her name, I want to hear all about her, like how did you all meet, do you know what type of ring she'd like, you know, all the good stuff."

Shuffling his posh chair closer to Maria's desk, Lionel was raring to go for a chance to speak about his girlfriend, his soon to be fiancé and wife, "Her name is Marsha Williams and she means the world to me, she is so beautiful, all I can truly say is, I'm a lucky guy." Thinking back to how they actually met, he smirked, "We met online actually."

Locked into Lionel's story, Maria in a softened voice filled with curiosity, leaned in closer, "Online, huh? How'd that happen? I'm afraid of online dating, too many crazies out there."

Sharing in the humor, Lionel continued, he understood Maria's concern but he had a different experience with Marsha, he was now about to ask for her hand in marriage. "I had been in San Antonio for about a year, after having moved my business here which didn't leave me much time to be social or even date but I wanted to. Unbeknownst to me, a buddy of mine created a profile for me on an online dating site. I didn't find out what was going on until I started getting emails from random women. I mentioned it to my buddy and he could barely contain himself. He finally admitted to his prank. He was communicating with the women he thought I might like and then he'd give them my actual email address. Being in the I.T. industry, I wasn't afraid of having a profile and I thought, hey, why not...I don't have anything to lose so I kept it up. While I did go out on a few interesting dates to say the least, I ended up meeting Marsha."

Needing to know more details, Maria probed further, "What type of business brought you here to San Antonio?"

By becoming more animated in answering the question, Maria perceived Lionel loved his job. "I'm a consultant, I consult on various computer-related issues. I deal with vulnerabilities within computer systems. Unfortunately for San Antonio but fortunate for me, this city is a hotbed for crooked cyber activity."

Maria interrupted, "See, I told you, a lot of crazies out there. So does she know you're going to propose and do you know what she may like in a ring?"

Happy to report to Maria, Lionel looked around as if what he was about to reveal was top-secret information, "She has no idea I'm ready to propose. I have been asking her certain questions here and there to see what she likes but not enough to clue her in, so I think I have a pretty good idea of what she wants. I'm ready to pick out a ring."

Maria concluded her fact-finding mission and led Lionel to the engagement section of the store where everyone in the area smiled at him because they knew what he was there for. He received a couple of pats on the back and several congratulatory high-fives.

After hours in the store, with Lionel negotiating back and forth with Maria, she found the ring Lionel would present to Marsha. They both knew it was perfect when Lionel had to hold back a tear, confirming what he felt in his heart, "Yes, this is it!"

Selecting a flawless diamond would bring attention to Lionel's ability to choose right, the sparkling symbol would signal achievement in his life.

Cupping the beautifully wrapped black box in his hand, he felt like he could conquer the world, he was ready to make Marsha his forever. He had found his good thing[8].

The Love Bug.

---

[8] **Proverbs 18:22**: *"Whoso findeth a wife findeth a good thing, and obtaineth favour of the LORD."*

NOTE FROM THE AUTHOR
Final Thoughts

Words cannot express how thrilled I am to still have you reading up to this point. **THANK YOU, THANK YOU!**

I was in the middle of writing two other books when *High Noon Justice* stopped me in my tracks. I kept hearing the first line in my head for weeks and I decided one day I was going to sit down and write out what I was hearing. Believe it or not, you've just finished reading the result of what I started that day and I pray you have enjoyed reading it. In addition, you've previewed an upcoming novel and I hope you will be on the lookout for its release.

At this time in my life, I feel like I'm scripture personified based upon Ephesians 2:10:

> *"For we are his workmanship, created in Christ Jesus unto good works, which God hath before ordained that we should walk in them."*

My dear brothers and sisters, my sweethearts, I truly believe, I'm walking out what He preordained for my life and I'm so grateful to have you on this journey with me. I'd love to hear your thoughts. Feel free to email me at shakirabelieves@gmail.com.

For more information about what's going on with me, for latest news and announcements, book updates, simply ready to believe and so much more, please head over to www.shakirabelieves.com and sign up.

One Last Thing...

If you have enjoyed this book and believe your friends and family would enjoy it as well, I'd be honored if you decided to spread the word and tell them about it.

I'd be forever grateful if you posted an online review where ever you hang out, whether by social media, Amazon, Goodreads, Smashwords, you get the idea.

Remember, no matter what it looks like, trusting God simply means believing against all else that everything is going to work out. I promise you, the sun will shine again.

All the best,

Shakira ♥

Shakira R. Thompson